PONNIYIN SELVAN BOOK 6

INFANT EMPEROR

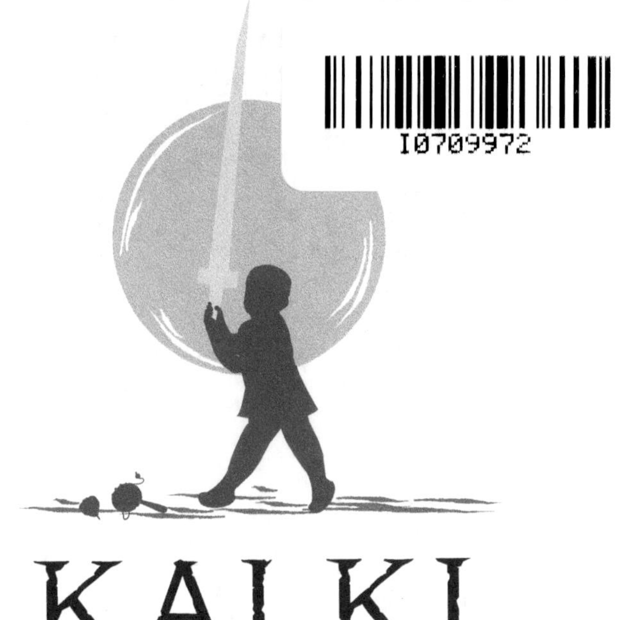

KALKI

TRANSLATED BY NANDINI KRISHNAN

ekadā

ekadā

First published in Tamil as *Ponniyin Selvan*

Published in English in 2025 by Ekadā, an imprint of Westland Books, a division of Nasadiya Technologies Private Limited

No. 269/2B, First Floor, 'Irai Arul', Vimalraj Street, Nethaji Nagar, Alapakkam Main Road, Maduravoyal, Chennai 600095

Westland, the Westland logo, Ekadā and the Ekadā logo are the trademarks of Nasadiya Technologies Private Limited, or its affiliates.

Translation copyright © Nandini Krishnan, 2025

ISBN: 9789371973588

10 9 8 7 6 5 4 3 2 1

This is a work of fiction. Names, characters, organisations, places, events and incidents are either products of the author's imagination or used fictitiously.

Typeset by Jojy Philip

Printed at

CONTENTS

INFANT EMPEROR

'Kalki' is the pen name of Ramaswamy Krishnamurthy (1899–1954), whose career in writing and journalism began as activism during the struggle for Indian independence. He served as editor of the popular Tamil magazine *Ananda Vikatan* before launching *Kalki*. The magazine—and eventually its founder—was named for the mythological tenth avatar of Vishnu to symbolise a vision to 'destroy regressive regimes, express radical thoughts, take readers into new directions, and create a new era'. Kalki wrote several novels, including *Parthiban Kanavu* and *Sivakamiyin Sabadam*, as well as political essays, film reviews, dance and music critiques and scholarly work.

Nandini Krishnan is the author of *Hitched: The Modern Woman and Arranged Marriage* and *Invisible Men: Inside India's Transmasculine Networks*. She has translated two of Perumal Murugan's works into English: *Estuary and Four Strokes of Luck*. She was shortlisted for the PEN Presents translation prize 2022 and the Ali Jawad Zaidi Memorial Prize for translation from Urdu 2022. She is an alumna of the Writer's Bloc playwrights' workshop by the Royal Court Theatre, London. Her novel-in-manuscript was a winner of the Caravan Writers of India Festival contest and showcased at the Writers of the World Festival, Paris, 2014.

1

VANATHI

If a poet were asked to describe the beauty of the Kodumbalur princess, he would compare her to the exquisite loveliness of the twilight hour. As the daylight fades, one feels a twinge of sadness, along with a sense of peace. As the last rays of the sun grow slimmer and slimmer until they vanish and darkness settles on the world, one feels tired. But then, all one has to do is turn one's eyes to the firmament, to see that the goddess of the skies has lit it up with millions upon millions of stars. They don't hurt the eye like the blazing sun. One can stare at the stars for as long as one desires, and derive joy from their twinkling forms. The full moon shines down upon the earth, and the world smiles back at this pearl in the sky.

True, lotuses gather their petals into themselves and fold up for the evening; but then, as if to give the stars a run for their money, millions of jasmine buds blossom into full blooms, intoxicating earth and sky with their fragrance. True, birds huddle in the trees to roost as the sun sets, and the world is deprived of their chirping and song. But then, the sounds of the semakkalam and nadaswaram from the temples soothe the ear. And these mingle with the music of the veena and yazh, strummed by the delicate fingers of the young women living in the various mansions in town.

The beauty of the Kodumbalur princess carried these shades of sorrow and joy, mingled and muddled into an indescribable aspect. As was her mien without, so was her mien within. There were times when she seemed to be the very embodiment of grief, as if Savitri[1] and Chandramati[2] had possessed her together. And there were other times when she danced and sang in a manner that made one think one was watching the apsaras Rambha and Urvashi performing in Indra's sabha. And yet others when she resembled Madhavi[3] in the first glow of love. But moments later, one would think she was Kannagi,[4] grieving for Kovalan. One might see her as Valli, whose heart was sick with love for Vadivelar, and who stood forlorn and waiting. At other times, she might be Deivanai, delirious with joy as she wed Kartikeya in such a grand ceremony as for the entire world of celestials to celebrate.[5]

Vanathi would go days without so much as the hint of a smile on her face. And there were days when she would laugh ceaselessly, the sound rising into the ether and filling the air with happiness.

It might be said that this contradiction in her nature, this swinging between extremes, was owed to the time she was born and the period in which she was raised. The story starts, in fact, before she was born. Even as her mother was pregnant with Vanathi, her father Kodumbalur Siriya Velaar had engaged in fierce wars. Rumours of victory and defeat would alternate with each other, bringing her mother relief and grief in turns.

Not long after her birth, Vanathi's mother passed away. Her father showered affection on the motherless child. But this love was not fated to last. The dauntless warrior that he was, Kodumbalur Siriya Velaar[6] could not be persuaded to stay away from the battlefield even for the sake of his toddling daughter. Once Veerapandiyan had been driven into hiding, Siriya Velaar chased the Lankan armies that had allied with the Pandiyas back to their island. He died on the battlefield at Eezham, and went down in history as 'Eezhaththu patta Siriya Velaar'.

Vanathi's life descended into gloom for some time after this. Only motherless girls who have been raised by their fathers can know this particular grief. The princess was pampered at the Kodumbalur palace, as everyone else tried to make up for the loss of her parents, but the void her father had left remained unfilled.

Of all the platitudes she endured, one man's words stood out. 'Don't worry, my child,' an elderly courtier had said. 'Your father will be reborn, from your own womb, as your own son. He will be so courageous as for the entire world to marvel at his feats on the battlefield.'

Those words took root in Vanathi's heart. She tried to assuage the sorrow of her father's absence with the anticipation of her unborn son's appearance in her life. She was largely successful. She fantasised constantly about how her son would look, how he would toddle, how he would walk and study and train and eventually go to war, what grand deeds he would accomplish, which faraway lands he would sail to and conquer ...

In her mind's eye, she saw him rush back from those victories to lay the spoils of war as tributes at his mother's feet. She saw his coronation ceremony, at which the greatest of kings arrived and bowed low before him. She saw his subjects swell like waves looking upon the full moon as he appeared before them. She saw a fleet of hundreds of ships sail behind him as he went on his missions of conquest and she heard him say in his baritone, 'Annaiye! All the pride and victories I have earned are owed to you and you alone!'

As a girl, she would stroke her aalilai-like midriff[7] and wonder whether this imagined child was already inside. Back in the day, everyone knew the story of the *Mahabharata*. Vanathi often thought of the way in which Kunti had birthed Karna. She wondered which god would descend from the heavens to bless her with this son. She did not think marriage was a prerequisite for birthing children. It was only after she came of age that she realised that she would have to acquire a husband to father the child. Even so, she didn't daydream about the future husband as she did about the future son.

It was only after she went to the Pazhaiyarai palace that her mind and heart underwent a change. Kundavai's sororal, sometimes maternal, concern and affection gave her solace, even as she could barely believe her good fortune. Kundavai's cultured manner, her choice of clothing and accessories, her graceful gait, her measured speech and her wit introduced Vanathi to a world she had never before known. The other princesses who had come to the palace from various kingdoms to serve as Kundavai's companions were envious of Vanathi, and this gave her a sense of validation—there must be something in her, some quality or aspect to which they aspired. But, even as she enjoyed their envy, her pleasant and generous nature led her to treat everyone with compassion and amity. Through all this, Vanathi remained preoccupied with dreams of her son-to-be.

It was at this time that she met Ponniyin Selvar. And with this encounter, the very foundations of the castles she had built in the air began to shake. All her life, she hadn't cared much for the man who would be her husband. He was an anonymous, asexual entity whose only purpose was to bring her beloved son into her life. But this untamed heart of hers had set itself on the man who was the object of the entire empire's love and affection. All fifty-six suzerain kings would line up to beg him to wed their daughters. Would he so much as throw a second glance at an orphan like her? She couldn't even dream of such a marriage. But once she had lost her heart to him, how could she marry anyone else? He would have his pick of princesses, while she would choose to remain unmarried. Once her prospects of marriage had disappeared, her unborn son vanished too. The castles she had built in the air came crumbling down. As these thoughts surged in her mind, her heart felt like it would burst from sorrow.

Kundavai, who had sensed the cause of this change in her friend's demeanour, showered love and encouragement upon Vanathi. She did her best to cheer the Kodumbalur princess up. She reassured her that her love was not limerent, that this marriage was not impossible. The predictions of the astrologer in Kudandai had fanned the flames. His declaration that she would have a son who would conquer the world triggered Vanathi's old dreams. This heightened her joys and deepened her sadness. Her yearning caused her unbearable pain. And the thought of her love being reciprocated, of a joyful union, filled her heart with such elation as to make her chest hurt from holding it all in. When either emotion exceeded its limit, she would collapse in a faint. These fits of unconsciousness were perhaps nature's way of saving her life, for no body was built to handle such volatility.

Her inner turmoil had been exacerbated by her stay in Thanjavur—the play she had watched, the terrible lament she had heard at night and the terrifying sight she had seen right after had all taken their toll on her. She had understood the intensity of the rivalry between the Kodumbalur and Pazhuvoor clans on that visit. She had also realised just how much influence the Pazuvettaraiyar brothers had in the running of the empire. Would they allow her dreams of marrying the prince to materialise? Even if the brothers had no objection, would the women of their family permit such an alliance? Would the Pazhuvoor Ilaiya Rani consent? Her status and the power she exercised over everyone was evident.

Every time she thought of Nandini, Vanathi's mind conjured the image of a beautiful cobra. She knew of the Pazhuvoor Rani's enmity with Ilaiya Piraatti. Would this hatred not extend to the latter's best friend? Why, that cobra might well spew its poison at Ponniyin Selvar. Was the form that had appeared before the ailing emperor, that so resembled Nandini, truly the Pazhuvoor Rani herself? Why had the emperor screamed in such agony, and spoken in such a terrified voice? Why was Ilaiya Piraatti adamant that she would not discuss the incident with her?

That brought her to another observation. Something in Ilaiya Piraatti had changed of late. She did not prattle on with Vanathi as she used to earlier. Kundavai Devi seemed to want to be alone more often these days. She seemed to be preoccupied with some tremendous worry. Perhaps it was anxiety over Ponniyin Selvar's well-being? Was that why she kept it hidden from Vanathi?

That day, too, Ilaiya Piraatti had disappeared all of a sudden. How the other girls teased Vanathi in Kundavai Devi's absence! And how cacophonous their laughter and singing were! These girls knew nothing of worry or sorrow. The world could come to an end, and they would still sing and dance. Vanathi had always disliked their jibes and teasing. And over the last couple of days, when she had been feeling as if she was at the bottom of an ocean of sadness, their nonsensical games had irritated her more than ever before. Now, she went in search of Ilaiya Piraatti. She learned that a sabha had gathered at Sembiyan Mahadevi's palace, and that Kundavai Devi had gone there. But by the time Vanathi reached the palace, the sabha had dispersed. Sembiyan Mahadevi was closeted with her son, having a private audience. For some reason, this discomfited Vanathi.

As she was leaving, she heard a commotion at the palace gates. A crowd had gathered there. Her need to be with Kundavai Devi now acquired a sense of urgency. She enquired with various maids, and learned that the Ilaiya Piraatti had met Azhvarkadiyaan privately, and then made for the lake in the palace gardens. These days, Kundavai did not seem to welcome any interruption of her solitude. Vanathi dithered, wondering whether she should follow the princess to the lake or not.

At that moment, Varini came running.

'Ponniyin Selvar has drowned at sea!' she cried, and then began to sob.

The other girls gasped and then joined in the wailing.

As for Vanathi, she seemed to feel nothing at all. Her mind was empty, her body numb. The other girls stared at her, and all their eyes seemed to say the same thing: 'Adi paavi! It was the misfortune and bad luck you carry with you that has caused our prince to drown!'

Vanathi could not bear the accusation, albeit an imagined one. She could no longer stand there. She raced to the palace garden. Her heart raced along with her.

The full import of the words 'The prince has drowned at sea' sank in. Even over the shock this news had triggered, a memory surfaced. For the last few days, every time she saw water, the prince's face appeared in it. Once, as she had stood on the shore, she had watched him walk out of the water. She had hurried to touch the form, but it had disappeared.

Now, she understood what this meant.

As the prince had drowned, his last thought had been of her. He was calling her. And the fool that she was, she had remained on shore, watching him.

Aha! What a mistake she had made! Well, there was no point trying to turn back time. What should she do now?

What an idiot she was! Did she even have to think about the course of action she should take? The lake that bordered the palace garden emptied into the Arisilaru. The Arisilaru merged into the sea. And at the bottom of the sea, the prince was waiting for her in a magical palace made of pearls and corals. What work did she have that was keeping her in this world, keeping her from going to him? Who was left for her in this world, anyway?

Once she had made up her mind, a sense of peace and well-being settled upon Vanathi's heart. Her panic abated. Her sorrow disappeared. Her anxiety vanished. She walked calmly to the edge of the lake, stepping down the marble stairs. She looked about herself. She could see a boat approaching from a distance. It was indeed Ilaiya Piraatti who was sitting inside. But who was the other occupant? Ah, it appeared to be the man whom they had first met at the house of the astrologer in Kudandai, the man who had taken a scroll to Lanka. It must be he who had brought the news of the prince's demise.

So, this was why Ilaiya Piraatti had slipped away. She had wanted to meet him and find out the details of what had transpired. She had left Vanathi behind to keep the news from her. Once Kundavai reached the shore, Vanathi would not be able to do as her heart desired. Ilaiya Piraatti would try to comfort her, and insist there was hope. She would prevent Vanathi from joining the prince. But, even so, was it right to leave without so much as saying goodbye to the princess who had showered unconditional love upon an orphan? Surely, she should at least thank her? No, no! She could not afford to wait.

Here, his face appeared in the water. Why, his entire body appeared. He was calling to her. He was smiling.

'All the obstacles in the way of my marrying you have been removed,' he said. 'Come to me.'

How could she linger now? Aha, she felt dizzy. Surely she was not going to faint! Well, it wouldn't be a problem, so long as she fainted in the water and not on shore.

Things went as Vanathi desired. It was the water she fell into. Her body and heart welcomed the cold water, a relief from their feverish state. Down, down, down she went. How long, how far, she had no idea. It might have been moments; it might have been aeons.

Ah, she had arrived at the wonder-world that was underwater. This must be Nagalokam, the abode of snakes. Aha, what beautiful palaces, with so many levels rising so high she couldn't see the terraces! How was the light that illuminated this underwater world clearly still so cool on the eyes? Perhaps the water had cooled the sun's rays?

How was the light so bright, though? Ah, it was bouncing off the walls of the palaces. No surprise, for the walls were made of gold and pearls and diamonds, and the rare snake-stone.

What was that crowd approaching her? Why, their entire forms were luminous, and their faces glowed! They must be from Devalokam! Was it not Nagalokam she had arrived in, then? Was it Devalokam?

And then, as if she was in a dream within a dream, a series of events occurred in quick succession. The new arrivals ushered her to a mandapam which had been ornately decorated. Ponniyin Selvar was standing there, a smile on his face. He greeted Vanathi. As the divine instruments played music and flowers fell upon them and mantras were chanted, the prince and Vanathi exchanged garlands and were wedded. Vanathi, overcome with joy, fell into a faint. It seemed she was unconscious for a long time, but then two strong arms reached for her. At first, she thought those were Ponniyin Selvar's arms. He had carried her and laid her on his lap. But then, she felt bangles against her forehead.

'Vanathi! Vanathi! What a thing to do!' a woman's voice cried.

It took an enormous effort for Vanathi to part her eyelids.

Kundavai's face was peering into hers.

'Akka! Akka! Did you attend my wedding? I couldn't spot you there …' Vanathi mumbled.

2

VANATHI REGAINS CONSCIOUSNESS

Vanathi fell back into a faint. Her eyes fluttered closed. And then, slowly, her consciousness began to return. She realised it was simply a hallucination that she had travelled to Nagalokam and Devalokam and married the prince. She remembered how she had heard the terrible news about Ponniyin Selvar, run to the garden and stood at the edge of the water, how she had felt dizzy and fallen into its depths.

And as the reality of it all hit her, she felt a sense of betrayal, the pain of a spear piercing her heart. She tried to open her eyes, but her lids felt too heavy. Who had lifted her out of the water and brought her safely to shore? It must have been Ilaiya Piraatti. Yes, it must have been Kundavai Devi, whom she had spotted in the boat some distance away.

Why had the princess saved her life? Why hadn't she let her sink to her death? She should take Ilaiya

Piraatti to task, and demand of her, 'Why did you save me from drowning?' Was this all the affection she had for her brother? Did she not understand that life without him was not worth living?

There, Ilaiya Piraatti was speaking. What was she saying? And to whom?

'She's delirious. She's blathering on. What a miracle it is that this fool survived! Imagine, if our boat had been a little further off! Or, if we hadn't spotted her falling into the water! My heart stops when I think of what might have happened!'

It might have been for the best. If only we hadn't spotted her, this poor girl's life would have ended happily. The Kodumbalur princess, who survived because of you, will have to endure much in the years to come ...'

Aha! Who was this, now? Who is speaking with so much concern for me? Ah, it was that young man. The man whom we met at the astrologer's home in Kudandai and later by the river! It must have been he who brought the news of the prince's drowning too ... what else are the two of them going to talk about? Let's listen in. I'm not able to open my eyes, but I can hear every word, Vanathi thought.

'What are you saying? Have you no heart? Are the hearts of all men made of stone?' said Ilaiya Piraatti's voice.

'What have I said to merit such judgement?'

'You said it would have been for the best if this girl had died! Isn't that enough to prove you have a heart of stone? Do you know how much trouble I'm taking to prepare her for her future?'

'Did you hear what she was saying in her delirium?'

'What did you hear?'

'I heard her say something about marrying the prince.'

'Yes, even in her delirium, she could only speak of him. Such is her love for him. It's taken root so deeply in her heart that he is on her mind even when she is unconscious.'

'And this love will be her undoing. She will suffer betrayal and agony.'

'Why do you say that? Which princess can you think of who would be more suited to the prince? Don't you know of the greatness of the Kodumbalur clan?'

'All too well. But we're talking at cross purposes. What's the point of her being a princess? Her heart's desire will not be realised.'

'Oh, it certainly will! It is not simply her heart's desire, but *my* heart's desire too. My plan, my decision.'

'It might be your decision, but it will not be heeded in this particular instance.'

'Why do you keep speaking like this? What you said just now, about the prince being safe in the Choodamani Viharam at Nagapattinam is true, isn't it?'

Aha! What is this wonderful news, now? The prince is safe? He is in the Choodamani Viharam at Nagapattinam?

How fortunate my ears are to have heard such a thing! What a good thing it has turned out to be that I survived, after all! I'm indebted to Ilaiya Piraatti for so much already, and here's one more thing to add to the list!

But then … what is he saying just now? It feels like molten lead is being poured into my ears!

'Ammani, it is true enough that the prince is safe. But how does that guarantee that this girl's dreams will come true? I am quite sure the prince will not marry her.'

'You are entitled to your opinions. However, there is one man in the world who will not cross the line I draw, who will not disobey my word. And he is my brother Arulmozhi Varman.'

'Ilavarasi! There is another such man. Yours truly.'

'In that case, why should there be any obstacle to my wish being fulfilled? Will the Pazhuvettaraiyar brothers get in the way of this too?'

'Now, that, I don't know. The prince's love for you knows no bounds, I'm aware of that. He will obey your word in every other matter. You see, he has no interest in ruling a kingdom. He refused the bejewelled crown of Lanka before my very eyes. Even so, he will fall in line if you force him to ascend the throne. But as for marrying this girl …'

'You say he won't consent? What does my darling friend lack? What fault could he possibly find in her to cast her aside? What fault can *you* find?'

'Ammani, I see no fault in this girl. Even if I did, I wouldn't believe it. Even the lowliest servant who walks within Ilaiya Piraatti's palace is as an apsara to me. The little rabbits in the garden of this palace are as Indra's Airavata[1] to me, well, superior, even. The prince, too, sees no fault. But isn't it possible that he has lost his heart to another woman?'

Aiyo! What cruel words! Why does this young man see fit to drive a spear into this heart that has already been wounded so often?

'O hero of the Vaanar clan! I don't understand what you're talking about. Why would you cast such aspersions against my brother?'

'These are not aspersions, ammani! I am simply telling you the truth. I'm telling you what I've seen with my own eyes and heard with my own ears.'

'Tell me more then! I am ready to hear anything at all, however hard it might be. But I want to know everything!'

'I mentioned a boatwoman called Poonguzhali, didn't I? She's the one who ferried me to Lanka. And it was she who saved me and the prince from drowning. And she also escorted the prince to the safety of the Choodamani Viharam. I would never have left the prince in the custody of Senthan Amudan alone. I don't have enough faith to do so in anyone but Poonguzhali. If that girl had a thousand lives, she would sacrifice every one of those to safeguard the prince.'

'So? A boatwoman is, after all, a boatwoman. Can she so much as dream of marrying a man who was born to rule the world? Can a little sparrow that is hopping about on the ground aspire to the eagle flying high above the world?'

'Why not? The little sparrow can aspire to the eagle flying high, and the eagle can swoop down to ogle the sparrow too.'

'If such a notion has entered my brother's head, it is my duty to dispel it! I have saved Arulmozhi from countless perils. And I will save him from this girl's clutches, from the web she has woven to entrap him ...'

'Does the fact that she is a boatwoman make her unworthy? Are clan and ancestry so very important? Isn't the blood that flows through a boatwoman's veins red too? Doesn't her heart beat as that of a princess born in a palace? If you think about it, a princess's love might also be tainted by the desire to become a queen, an empress even. Whereas that boatwoman's love is unsullied, pure. This is what the prince believes. Why should anyone else stand in the way? Now ... let's take my case, for instance. If I were to tear my heart open and show you what is within ...'

'Oh, no, no, please, no, thank you. Let whatever is within your heart stay safe right there. That would be for the best. Love and lust are all very well for commoners, but the lot of those who were born to rule is quite different. They *must* marry into royalty. They cannot allow themselves to be swayed. One little slip could set off a plague. Why, it's happened in my own family. In my father's youth ... when there appeared to be little chance of his being crowned emperor ... he made exactly the same mistake. A tribal girl from a forest had ... but why am I telling you all this now? This girl is regaining consciousness too. Her eyelids are fluttering, do you see? Do you have nothing else to say? You said you had several narrow escapes in Eezha Naadu, didn't you? Tell me about those!'

'Yes, indeed, ilavarasi! Once the prince had rejected the Lankan throne and crown, we were returning to the house in Anuradhapuram where we were to stay the night. As we were walking by a building, the front portion of a balcony broke off and came crashing down. If we'd been there an instant longer, it would have fallen on our heads and we would have been buried alive. Literally a moment before it fell, a woman appeared from nowhere and gestured to the prince urgently. I don't know who she is, but the prince seemed to know her. Please don't get all suspicious now, ammani! She is an elderly woman.'

'How old?'

'Old enough to be the prince's mother. And she is deaf-mute too.'

'What? What did you say?'

'She is an old woman, seems to have been deaf-mute from birth. She must be at least forty-five years old.'

'Aiya! You saw one such woman in Eezha Naadu, you say? Please tell me more! Do you know anything about her? Her early years? Where was she born?'

'An island off the coast of Eezham.'

The princess seemed beside herself, as she asked, 'Aiya! Please tell me more! How did she look?'

'Ammani! I found something quite strange about her appearance. Something extraordinary. But I hesitate to tell you.'

'Please don't hesitate. Tell me right away!'

'She looks exactly like a woman I've seen in Chozha Naadu. The only difference is that the lady who came to our rescue in Eezha Naadu was so much older. She wore no silks and ornaments, and her hair was loose. But she had the very same face, the very same figure … for a moment, I thought my eyes were playing a trick on me. I thought … I thought …'

'Aiya, who is that woman? The woman from Chozha Naadu, I mean, the one she resembles?'

'Ilavarasi, are you not able to guess?'

'Is it me? Vanathi? My mother in the Thanjavur palace?'

'None of the above.'

'Pazhuvoor Ilaiya Rani Nandini?'

'Yes, Nandini.'

'Oh, God! This means my suspicions were right.'

'What did you suspect?'

'I suspected that the woman I considered viler than a venomous snake might be my older sister. And what you have just told me affirms that this is indeed the case. Oh, is there anything crueller than fate? This is evidence of what a grave error it is for a royal to marry someone of unknown ancestry!'

'Ammani! I am not a man of unknown ancestry. My ancestors ruled Tamizhagam for three hundred years. They threw Chera and Chozha and Pandiya kings in prison! I might not have a kingdom, but I have a sword in my hands and strength in my shoulders and courage in my heart and ...'

'Aiya! I'll listen to your paeans to yourself in some time. But there are things that need immediate attention. I need your help. You will help me, won't you?'

'If I had a thousand lives, I would give them all up for you.'

'You must be that boatwoman Poonguzhali's twin, then. All right, all right, enough of this talk. Here, look, this girl is about to open her eyes.'

Yes, Vanathi had indeed regained full consciousness. There was a newfound strength in her body. Various thoughts jostled for space in her head. She decided she had to stay alive until she had proven to the prince that her love was deeper and more sincere than that of the boatwoman. At the same time, she remembered the sights she had seen and the lament she had heard in the emperor's bedchamber in Thanjavur. It was all beginning to make sense now.

The moment Vanathi opened her eyes, Ilaiya Piraatti said tenderly, 'Kanne! Are you all right?'

'I'm fine. Akka! I'm sorry, I've put you to a lot of trouble.'

At this moment, Azhvarkadiyaan entered the scene and said, 'I'm afraid I'm going to put you to a lot of trouble too. Devi! There's a teeming crowd and grand commotion at the entrance to the palace. The people of Chozha Naadu are beside themselves with rage and grief over the news they've heard about the prince. Unless you come right away, to talk to them and calm them down, things will get out of hand!'

$$3$$

THE PRIME MINISTER'S ARRIVAL

The streets of Pazhaiyarai were witnessing such a commotion as there had never been before. Swarms of people were making for the section of the town that housed the royal palaces. Men and women, youth and old people, little boys and girls, Shaivites and Vaishnavites, Buddhists and Jains and Kalamukhas were all swept together in that crowd. They wailed and wept, and many cursed the Pazhuvettaraiyar brothers.

Some of the young men carried batons. Every now and again, they would clash them against each other and chant, 'May these land on the Pazhuvettaraiyars' heads!' Some whispered the words, and some shouted them out. The Kalamukhas were among the latter.

The royal palaces of Pazhaiyarai all had crescent-shaped front yards. They also had large verandahs where people could assemble for special occasions. High walls ran around each palace, enveloping these spaces. The walls had three entrances, and guards and servants stood at each.

The crowd was making for the palace that housed Periya Piraatti and Ilaiya Piraatti. People surged towards each of the entrances, and the numbers grew with every instant. The guards admitted the two messengers from Thanjavur and their escort alone. They barred the townspeople from entering. But this did not stop them for long.

Soon enough, cries of 'Go inside! Go inside!' rose from the crowd.

Those at the front were pushed by the force of those behind them, and the sea of people behaved quite like the ocean, wave after wave giving momentum to the water until the first ripples breached the sand. And so, the townspeople swept the guards along as they breached the entrances, and soon, it was as though the floodgates had opened, allowing the Kaveri to surge through. Thousands upon thousands assembled in the front verandah of the palace.

And it was the noise they made that alerted Sembiyan Mahadevi to the emergency as she was talking to her son. She cut short her argument and went to the balcony to see what was happening. She greeted the crowd with folded hands. When they saw the matriarch, her face glowing with devotion to Shiva, her mien the very essence of peace, the townspeople began to calm down. It was not long before silence reigned in the hall.

'Thaaye! Where is our prince? Where is Ponniyin Selvar? Where is Arulmozhi Varmar, dearer to you than life itself?' someone shouted.

With that, the silence was broken, and the crowd grew even louder and more flustered than they had been before Periya Piraatti's appearance.

The matriarch stood stupefied, not understanding a thing. She realised something terrible had happened to the prince whom everyone in the empire adored. What could have happened? And how? Had the Pazhuvettaraiyar brothers hatched a plot and set in motion events that would bring indelible infamy upon Madurantakan and the Chozha clan?

By this time, the two messengers had elbowed their way to the front of the crowd.

One of the guards who had escorted them bowed and said, 'Perumaatti! These men bring important news from Thanjavur!'

Sembiyan Mahadevi raised a hand to call for silence from the crowd, and then looked at the two men and asked, 'What news do you bring?'

'Thaaye! We are the unfortunate bearers of devastating news. In accordance with the Chakravarti's orders, Arulmozhi Varmar had boarded a ship from Lanka to Kodikkarai. The ship was caught in a tempest. A second ship that was escorting the first was wrecked at sea. The prince jumped into the water to save those aboard. He has not been seen since. Search parties have been sent out to scour the seas and comb the sands for him. The emperor and empress are broken by this news. The Chakravarti has sent us here to ask that you, Madurantaka Devar and Ilaiya Piraatti leave for Thanjavur right away.'

The news hit Sembiyan Mahadevi and the assembled crowd simultaneously. Tears started cascading down the matriarch's cheeks, and the sight of her sobbing helplessly sent a fresh lament through the townspeople.

Someone at the front of the crowd cried, 'Thaaye! You must not go to Thanjavur! Neither must Ilaiya Piraatti! Please ask the emperor to come back here!'

'It is a lie that Ponniyin Selvar drowned at sea! The Pazhuvettaraiyar brothers must have assassinated him!'

That was someone else.

'Madurantakar should not go to Thanjai either! He must stay right here!'

'Where is Ilaiya Piraatti? We want to see her!'

'Yes! We want the princess!'

'Where is Kundavai Devi?'

Sembiyan Mahadevi turned to one of the servant girls and ordered her to fetch Ilaiya Piraatti.

This was when Azhvarkadiyaan, who was in the crowd, had slipped away. He had found his usual shortcut and approached Kundavai Devi as she was reviving Vanathi. He had heard her last words to Vandiyadevan as he arrived, and told them what was happening in the palace.

Ilaiya Piraatti left Vanathi to the ministrations of the maids, and hurried to the balcony where her great-aunt stood. When she emerged on to it, she saw the tears in Sembiyan Mahadevi's eyes, and the sight made her well up too. When the crowd saw Kundavai Devi in tears, they took it as confirmation of their worst fears.

'The Pazhuvettaraiyar brothers have assassinated our prince! We must avenge this!'

'The Pazhuvettaraiyar brothers have imprisoned the emperor! We must free him and bring him here! Command us, princess, and we will march on Thanjai right away!'

As she heard the townspeople cry out to her, Kundavai Devi's mind raced. She must not give away the fact that the prince was alive. However, she needed to mollify the crowd and send them home. An idea occurred to her.

She wiped away her tears and looked at the first row of people assembled below the balcony. Azhvarkadiyaan and Vandiyadevan had made their way to the verandah too. Ilaiya Piraatti gestured to Azhvarkadiyaan to come upstairs. When he joined her, she whispered something to him.

Azhvarkadiyaan raised his arms for silence, and then said in a stentorian voice:

'Ilaiya Piraatti is not convinced that Ponniyin Selvar has died at sea. Our princess believes that just as Kaveri Amman once carried our prince to safety, so must the Samudra Raja. She has consulted a nimithakaaran, who has affirmed this. Ilaiya Piraatti will make all arrangements to find the prince. She asks that you put your minds to rest and return home.'

At this, a rumble rose from the crowd, almost a sigh of discontent.

'Where is this nimithakaaran? We want to hear the good news from him with our own ears!' someone said.

Vandiyadevan decided this was the moment to act, and ran up to the balcony. He took his place by Azhvarkadiyaan and said, 'It is true that the stars were aligned against the prince. But there was no danger to his life. He will return to us soon!'

'How do *you* know this?' someone shouted.

'I'm a nimithakaaran. I studied the planets and stars, and read the signs.'

'Lies! You're a liar! You're not a nimithakaaran! You're a spy!' the same person cried.

Vandiyadevan searched for the source of the voice, and landed on a face he recognised as that of the physician's son.

'You madman! You call me a spy? You dare call me a spy? If I'm a spy, on whose behalf am I spying?' he demanded.

'The Pazhuvettaraiyars!' the physician's son retorted right away.

'What did you say?' Vandiyadevan roared.

About twelve feet separated the balcony from the verandah below. Paying this no mind, Vandiyadevan leapt down, aiming right for the physician's son. He landed on his target and pushed him to the ground, where the two men began to wrestle.

We all know that no one, under any circumstance and at any point of time, has ever been able to resist a good fight. The crowd made space for the wrestlers and stepped back to gawk at the duel. The smaller assembly in the balcony peered down anxiously.

Most of the townspeople were too far back to understand what was happening, but they shouted louder than ever and jostled each other to surge forward.

Just then, a conch blew and trumpets sounded, even as a crier's voice bellowed, 'The prime minister is here! Prime Minister Aniruddha Brahmarayar has arrived! Make way, make way!'

The crowd parted at once.

4

ANIRUDDHAR'S PLEA

The palanquin that bore Prime Minister Aniruddha Brahmarayar parted the crowd as it hurried to the front of the hall. The people on either side bowed low as it passed. Several began to speak to him of their worries about the prince. The prime minister raised a hand as a sign of both reassurance and blessing, as he passed them by. The bearers set the palanquin down right under the balcony.

The prime minister stepped out and folded his hands in greeting to Periya Piraatti and the princess.

He then turned to the wrestling duel that was under way. Vandiyadevan and Pinagapani were oblivious to what was happening around them, engaged in the fight as they were.

Azhvarkadiyaan had descended the stairs by now and whispered something into the prime minister's ear.

Aniruddha Brahmarayar then turned to the soldiers who had escorted him and said, 'Throw these two troublemakers in prison!'

Azhvarkadiyaan accompanied the soldiers as they muscled their way through the crowd and hauled the two men up. He gestured at Vandiyadevan, who realised the arrest was part of a plan and allowed himself to be led away without resisting.

Aniruddhar then made his way to the balcony, and addressed the townspeople from there. 'I am aware of your anxiety and anger. The emperor and his queens are steeped in sorrow, just as you are. I ask that you do not do anything to exacerbate their problems. All arrangements have been made for the prince's rescue. I ask that you all return home calmly. Rest assured that our prince will return.'

'We want to see the emperor! He must return to Pazhaiyarai!'

'What has become of our men in Lanka?'

Various voices from the audience shot more questions at the prime minister, who raised his hand for silence and said, 'The emperor is safe in the Thanjavur palace. The Velakkaara Army stands guard day and night. I will personally escort the emperor to this town when the time is right. You need not worry about our men in Lanka either. The war in Eezham has ended with a decisive victory for us. Your war heroes will return to Chozha Naadu very soon.'

The crowd roared in delight at this news.

The people shouted slogans in praise of Sundara Chozhar and Aniruddha Brahmarayar as they began to disperse.

The prime minister then turned to Sembiyan Mahadevi and said, 'Devi, I have crucial matters to discuss with you. May we go into the palace?' He said to the princess, 'Amma, I will come to see you later.'[1] Kundavai understood she was being dismissed, and repaired to her quarters.

Several worries were taking root in Kundavai's mind now. If there was anyone in the entire empire of whom the princess was afraid, it was Aniruddha Brahmarayar. Not only was he eagle-eyed, he had a pair of eyes in the back of his head to boot. It was as if all those eyes could not only see what was before them but also read the minds and hearts of everyone they fell upon.

How much he knew, how much he didn't, what one might confide in him, what should be kept from him ... Ilaiya Piraatti could never figure out.

She had been vexed by his order to arrest the Vaanar scion along with Pinagapani. But she could not show her feelings. She could not speak up on Vandiyadevan's behalf in front of an audience. Well, he had said he would see her later. Let him come, she would put him in his place, she thought angrily, as she went to her antapuram.

Sembiyan Mahadevi commanded the respect of everyone in the empire, and the prime minister was no exception.

However, Periya Piraatti felt intimidated by him on this particular occasion. She waited for him to be seated before she sat down.

'Aiya! For some time now, I feel thunderbolt after thunderbolt is being launched at me. Every bit of news I hear leaves me ever more devastated. Do you bring such news too? Or, do you have words that will be of solace to me?'

'Ammani! Please forgive me, but I'm unable to answer your question. I suppose it depends on how you take the news I bring,' the prime minister said.

'Is the news about Ponniyin Selvan true, aiya? I'm not able to bring myself to believe it. What hopes we had for Arulmozhi Varman! How often we've heard it said that he was born to rule the entire world!'

'Perumaatti! It *is* true that you've told me about the astrologers making such a prediction. I have never contradicted you. But I have never echoed those sentiments either.'

'Well, that's beside the point. But tell me, are you sure that Samudra Raja has stolen Ponniyin Selvan from us?'

'How can I be sure of that, thaaye? All I am sure of is that such news has spread across the land.'

'If it is proven true, what will become of Chozha Naadu? What terrible things lie in store for us?'

'Those terrible things will not lie in wait until there is confirmation of the news, I think ...'

'Yes, yes, rumours are enough to set off a disaster. I've never seen a mob break into the palace in Pazhaiyarai before ...'

'Please don't think such an incident is restricted to Pazhaiyarai. Thanjavur has been simmering since yesterday. The Velakkaara Army has refused to budge from the emperor's palace. People poured into the fort in a tidal wave and surrounded the Pazhuvettaraiyar brothers' palaces. Elephants in musth had to be set on them to get them to scatter!'

'Aiyo! What a thing to happen! What frightening news you bring!'

'It is a good thing Madurantakar returned to Pazhaiyarai. Or he would have been subject to the same accusations as the Pazhuvettaraiyars.'

'Aiya, you would be shocked by the change that has come over Madurantakan.'

'No, I wouldn't be shocked, thaaye. I have known of this for some time.'

'And yet you made no effort to change his mind! Well, come up with something at least now! Tell me how we can undo this.'

'Amma, I don't see a need to change Madurantakan's mind. I am here to speak on his behalf.'

'What do you mean? I don't understand, aiya!'

'Ammani! Madurantakar believes the Chozha throne is his birthright. He desires to inherit the empire from the Chakravarti. That is fair. He is justified in thinking it should be his. The desire has taken deep root in his heart. Nothing good will come of trying to stop it. It would be most prudent to make that dream come true.'

'Aiyo! What a thing to say! Have you joined the ranks of the traitors too? What times are upon us!'

'Perumaatti, I would not so much as dream of committing treason. I am here on the orders of the emperor. I carry a request from him to you, an appeal from Sundara Chozhar himself. Madurantakar desires the throne. The Pazhuvettaraiyar brothers are conspiring to ensure he inherits the empire. But the emperor himself wants to crown him his heir. And he has sent me here expressly to seek your permission.'

'The emperor can want anything, but he will never have my permission for this! I will never consent to anything that goes against my husband's wishes. O Prime Minister, you have known the farthest limits of the sea of knowledge! How were you able to bring yourself to tell me something that flouts every custom, emperor's command or not? There are some truths that are known only to you and me, truths that have to do with the rightful inheritance of the Chozha throne ... have you forgotten them all?'

'Ammani! I have forgotten nothing. And I also know truths that you are unaware of. This is why I have come to you as the emperor's messenger.'

'Aiya, the entire world is aware of your acumen and shrewdness. Please don't use your sophistry against a woman.'

'Perumaatti! I am not here to argue with you. Or to exercise my aptitude at managing situations. I am simply here to make a plea. I am here to grovel before you, and pray that you grace us with a decision that would save our beloved empire from grave danger.'

'Reserve your prayers for my Shiva Peruman or the Vishnu Murti you prefer.'

'Yes, thaaye, if you will not grace us with your generosity, it will be up to Hari and Haran to save this land.'

'What is this grave danger you speak of? And how can it be averted by Madurantakan ascending the throne?'

'Do listen to what I have to say, Perumaatti. Just as the people of this town rose in rage, there will be unrest in every city from Kanchipuram to Rameshwaram. And it will not end there. I know that Boothi Vikrama Kesari is marching from Lanka with an army in tow. When the news of Arulmozhi Varman reaches Aditya Karikaralan, he will march on Thanjai with the entire army he commands. The Pazhuvettaraiyar brothers and the suzerain kings who have allied with them are already gathering their armies. There will be a civil war here, as there was between the Kauravas and Pandavas, for the right to rule. All your near and dear ones will perish. Are you going to stand by and watch?'

'Aiya! O Prime Minister, who is endowed with intelligence and acumen! I have no near and dear ones. You must have heard of Shankara, a great soul born in the northern lands. He has sung:

Matacha Parvati Devi
Pitadevo Maheshwara:
Bandhavah: Shiva bhaktaacha

'And I say, as he did, that my mother is Parvati Devi, my father is Paramashiva, my near and dear ones are the devotees, who are their children, and that I have no other connections to this world.'

'Ammani! Let me remind you of the fourth line from the same shloka:

Swadesho Bhuvanatrayam

'It is Shankara who said this, that the land into which we are born are our three worlds. Will you stand by and watch as your own land is destroyed by infighting?'

'My own land is dearer to me than all three worlds, it is true. But is Chozha Naadu, this mere sliver of land, my own land? No. Never. My own land stretches right up to the mountain Kailasha. If I have no place in Chozha Naadu, I will head to Kashi. Or to Kashmir, or Kailasha. I have been dreaming of this pilgrimage for a very long time, and I would be grateful for your help.'

'Thaaye! I do accept your contention that our land stretches from Tirikonamalai to the glaciers in the northernmost reaches of Bharat. But even this swathe of land is in grave danger. The Pathans, Turks, Mughals and Arabs are marching in search of lands to conquer. Just as the Yavanas[2] and Hunas[3] arrived with arms a thousand years ago, these people who belong to a new religion now plan to attack us. Their religion is a strange one. They believe it is a virtue to raze temples and destroy idols. Ammani! There are no emperors in the north powerful enough to stop them. I have been dreaming that our Chozha heroes will conquer the lands beyond the Ganga, why the Himalayas themselves, and stop this marauding crowd from desecrating our temples. Please help this dream come true! Please consent to Madurantakar being designated crown prince, and prevent a war over inheritance!'

Sembiyan Mahadevi sat in silent contemplation for some time. Then, she said, 'Aiya! You have spoken of things beyond my comprehension and caused me great consternation. It is only Sarveshwara who can prevent these marauders from marching on us, not a woman who is far from worldly. I will never forget the words my husband spoke before he left for his heavenly abode. And I will never go against them either.'

'In that case, I am compelled to tell you a truth that you do not know,' Aniruddhar said.

At that moment, Madurantakan barged in without ceremony, shouting, 'Amma! What is this I hear? That Arulmozhi Varman has drowned at sea?'

'Perumaatti! Please console your son. I will return at a more suitable time to tell you what I was going to say,' the prime minister said, and took his leave.

The moment Aniruddha Brahmarayar had crossed the threshold, Madurantakan said, 'That man who's leaving now, he's my foremost enemy! He's come to poison your mind, even as I sit right here, hasn't he?'

His angry words were just loud enough for Aniruddhar to catch.

5

KUNDAVAI IN TORMENT

Prime Minister Aniruddha Brahmarayar arrived at Kundavai's palace.

The princess got to her feet the moment she saw him, and bowed low before him.

'May you marry a man who is as courageous as he is kind, and live a long and happy life with him,' Aniruddhar said in blessing.

'Aiya! Of all the things you might wish for me at a time like this!'

'I'm an old man, and used to wishing this on young women. What would you prefer that I said?'

'All of us are anxious about my beloved father's health. The entire empire is in a state over Arulmozhi Varmar ...'

'But I see no sign of anxiety about your brother on your face, thaaye!'

'I was born into a clan of heroes. Would you have me sobbing and wailing like everyone else at the scent of danger?'

'No, never. All I ask is that the princess offer solace to those like me, who are lacking in heroism.'

'Acharya! You ask that *I* offer *you* solace? Why, you have a heart as hard as diamond, which would stand staunch and strong even if the world were to end!'

'And yet you've made that very heart break, amma! The ladies of the antapuram were meant for joyous, carefree lives, spent singing and dancing. You chose to cast that aside and interfere in matters of the state. And look what a disaster that has brought upon us!'

'Aiyo! What an accusation to make! In which matter of state did I interfere? And what disaster was caused by it?'

'I had said Ponniyin Selvan must stay on in Lanka for the time being. But you sent a scroll demanding that he leave right away. Who would choose to obey this old man if that involved going against your wishes? You see what a devastating consequence your letter has had? The sea has carried away the prince who was dearer than life itself to the subjects of this empire. You saw the mob that broke its way into the palace this morning. There have been such incidents across the empire. Aren't you to blame for this commotion?'

'You claim Arulmozhi Varman left from Lanka after reading my letter? Are you not aware that the Pazhuvettaraiyar brothers sent two ships to arrest Ponniyin Selvan?'

'I know, amma, I know! If he had been prompted only by that one message, the blame for his loss would have been placed on those brothers. Both their ships were wrecked in the storm. But, if they were to say he was coming to see you because of the scroll you sent, how would anyone refute it?'

'Aiya, how did you know I had sent him a scroll? How do the Pazhuvettaraiyar brothers know?'

'What a question! How do *we* know? Why, the entire world knows! Your messenger got himself arrested practically on arrival. And so, the entire army in Lanka knows. And thanks to the physician's son who accompanied him to Kodikkarai, everyone in Chozha Naadu knows too. Your secret mission is now public knowledge. This is why our elders have said women should not poke their noses into governance.'

Kundavai was stunned into silence for some time. She didn't know how to respond. The prime minister had cornered her. There was some truth in what he'd said.

She felt angry with the scion of the Vaanar clan. She was aware that he had a propensity for impulsive behaviour and a knack for getting himself into scrapes. But he had failed to keep such a crucial mission secret! She would give him a piece of her mind when she saw him. That reminded her that he had been thrown into prison on the prime minister's orders. What a mess he had made for himself, and for her too! Why hadn't he exercised some self-control? So what if the physician's son saw fit to provoke him? Why had he jumped off the balcony to take that fool on in a duel?

'Aiya! I have a request to make. You must be so generous as to grant it!'

'Devi! I'm at your command. Who has the power to overrule you in this empire?'

'When you arrived at the palace, two men were wrestling each other. You ordered that they be imprisoned.'

'They committed an unforgivable crime. How dare they start a fight in the palace, in the presence of our maharani? And at this time, when the entire town was simmering with rage! What if everyone had got involved and started throwing punches to give vent to that anger? All it takes for a forest fire to destroy an entire swathe of ancient woodland is a single spark.'

'You're right, aiya. They did commit an unforgivable crime. But I beg of you to pardon and release one of those men.'

'And who is this man who has the great fortune and honour of receiving such grace from the princess?'

'The man I sent as my messenger to Lanka.'

'Ha! It's a case of the fruit falling right into the milk bowl!'

'Why do you say that?'

'I had intended to arrest that messenger. And he has contrived to get himself imprisoned with no effort on my part.'

'But why did you intend to arrest him? For what crime?'

'Thaaye! He has been accused of a terrible crime!'

'Which is ...?'

'That it was he who pushed Ponniyin Selvan into the water, and caused his drowning!'

'What horrible words! Who has accused him of such a crime?'

'Several witnesses. Parthibendran, who was on board the same ship as the prince, blames him. The Pazhuvettaraiyar brothers say it is possible. I suspect him too.'

'Acharya! Are you telling me you suspect that I dispatched an assassin to kill my little brother?'

'Not on my life, thaaye! You sent him in the belief that he was trustworthy. But you might have been mistaken, no? It is possible that he is an enemy spy, isn't it?'

'No, absolutely not! Aditya Karikalan sent him to me. He wrote that he could be trusted unconditionally.'

'And isn't it possible Aditya Karikalan had been taken in too? Or that the messenger had a change of heart on the way? When I was entering, I heard the man downstairs accuse the man on the balcony of being a spy. What was that about, amma?'

'The man on the balcony is the messenger my older brother sent—Vallavarayan Vandiyadevan of the Vaanar clan. The man downstairs was the physician's son, Pinagapani. He accused Vandiyadevan of being the Pazhuvettaraiyar brothers' spy! What lunacy!'

'Why is it not possible, thaaye?'

'Well, because he escaped the clutches of the Pazhuvettaraiyar brothers. He was in their palace, and was going to be thrown into the dungeon, but he gave them the slip. They then sent a whole army of soldiers to retrieve him, but were unsuccessful.'

'How did he get his hands on their signet ring?'

'That vengeant rakshashi, that mayamohini, the venomous snake ... do forgive me for these epithets ... I speak of the Pazhuvoor Ilaiya Rani. She gave it to him.'

'I'm glad you're aware of this already. You would not have believed me if I had told you. Well, so let's say this man is not spying for the Pazhuvettaraiyar brothers. But he could be the Pazhuvoor Rani's spy, couldn't he?'

'How is that possible?'

'I'll tell you how. Vandiyadevan—the secret messenger you sent to Lanka—ran into the Pazhuvoor Rani outside the Thanjavur palace. He received her ring, and went on to meet her in the antapuram of the palace. The Pazhuvoor Ilaiya Rani hid him in the subterranean treasury and then sent him on his way through a secret passage. She knew he was carrying a message for you. On his way back from Lanka, they met at the bank of the Arichandra[1] river. Vandiyadevan could have returned the ring if he had no more use for it. And yet it was with him. What are your thoughts on this, amma? Can you trust your messenger unconditionally in spite of all this?'

Now, Kundavai's heart was genuinely tormented. She was so confused, she didn't know quite what to believe.

6

SPYING ON A SPY

Aniruddha Brahmarayar addressed the princess, who had fallen silent, and asked, 'Why won't you speak, thaaye? Do you still trust Vandiyadevan?'

'Aiya, you're an icon among administrators. What can I say? If you were to go on in this vein for a while, you'll ensure I can't even trust myself,' the princess said.

'Such are the times we live in, amma! It isn't easy to tell whom one can trust and whom one can't these days. We are surrounded by enemies and secret conspiracies,' the prime minister said.

'And yet one feels there can be no secret you don't know, no conspiracy you haven't discovered. How did you learn so much about my messenger?' Kundavai asked.

'Ammani, I have a thousand eyes and two thousand ears. They're spread across the land. I have men in the Pazhuvoor palace and among the Pazhuvoor Ilaiya

Rani's bodyguards, I have men who travel from town to town like Azhvarkadiyaan, and I believe nothing can happen in any of our neighbouring kingdoms without my hearing of it. Yet, who can tell? Someone just might trick me too. There might be secrets of which I will forever remain unaware.'

Kundavai wondered whether he knew that Ponniyin Selvan was in the Choodamani Vihara. It took some effort on her part to hide this suspicion.

'Aiya, you might be right on every other count, but I'm not able to believe that the scion of the Vaanar clan could be a spy commissioned by the Pazhuvoor Rani. Please do release him!'

'Think carefully, amma. That woman Nandini possesses some mysterious power. Madurantakan cast aside his Shiva bhakti for dreams of an empire after he fell into her trap. Sambuvarayar's son Kandamaaran has taken an olai from her to Aditya Karikalan. Parthibendran, who was a sworn enemy of the Pazhuvettaraiyar brothers, is now a slave to Nandini's whims. He has volunteered to convince Aditya Karikalan that it would be best to split the empire into two, one half for Madurantakan and one half for Adityan.'

'What! Split the empire? How much our ancestors have striven and sacrificed to bring all these lands together under one flag! Split *that* empire?'

'You don't want to see the empire split in two. Neither do I. Thaaye! If someone had suggested this idea to Parthibendran ten days ago, he would have seethed and raged. And yet, he is one of its advocates now.'

'How bizarre! What is this magical power that the Pazhuvoor Rani has, do you think?'

'Ilavarasi, I was planning to ask you that same question. And you pose it to me! But leave that aside for now. How are you so certain that Vandiyadevan alone is exempt from her charms?'

'Aiya, I'm not able to articulate my reasons for this belief. They say the heart is its own witness. And my heart is certain, for some reason, that this Vaanar hero will not brook such thoughts of betrayal.'

'Then, let's put that to the test, amma.'

'What test do you propose, aiya?'

'We must send a messenger to Kanchi right away. We must send an olai through someone whom Adityan trusts implicitly.'

'Saying what?'

'Moments ago, you referred to Nandini as a venomous snake and asked for my forgiveness. But truth be told, she is far more vile than a venomous snake. She is plotting to destroy the Chozha clan, to wrench it out by the roots.'

'Kadavule! What an awful thought!' Kundavai said. The thoughts that arose in her mind caused great turbulence in her heart.

'She has instigated Sambuvarayar to invite Aditya Karikalan to the Kadambur palace. She's been speaking of how they should marry him off to one of Sambuvarayar's daughters as well as to one of Pazhuvettaraiyar's daughters. I believe she intends to discuss the splitting of the empire and its governance there too. And these are things I have heard from various sources. Yet, who knows what she has kept to herself? Who knows what her final goal is, what thoughts are running through her mind? I, who pride myself on knowing everything, am not able to read her mind.'

'And what do you think we should do about this, aiya?'

'We must find a way to prevent Aditya Karikalan from going to the Kadambur palace. We must send an olai through Vandiyadevan to warn him. And if Aditya Karikalan were to go against our wishes, Vandiyadevan must accompany him to Kadambur. He must stay as close to him as his shadow, and guard Adityan with his life. He should afford Adityan no opportunity to meet Nandini alone.'

Kundavai sighed. She knew the prime minister had weighed every word he had spoken. Was he aware of everything that she knew, or was he speaking solely from his concern for the sanctity of the empire? She couldn't tell.

'Aiya, why do you think it is so very important to prevent them from meeting each other?'

'Ammani, some of Veerapandiyan's Abathuthavigal have sworn an oath to destroy the Chozha clan. New gold coins, fresh off Periya Pazhuvettaraiyar's mint, have been finding their way to them. Need I say more?'

'No,' Kundavai mumbled.

She thought of the prince, who was fighting off his fever at Choodamani Vihara. Ponniyin Selvan could be in more danger than she had realised.

'Aiya! It is a blessing that you are the prime minister of Chozha Naadu at this time, when disaster upon disaster is being visited upon us! What arrangements have you made with regard to my younger brother?' she asked.

'I have asked that every Shiva and Vishnu temple in the empire conduct special prayers for the safe return of the prince. There will be prayers in the Buddhist and Jain temples too. The monks at the Choodamani Vihara in Nagapattinam have organised a series of rituals. Can you think of anything else?'

Kundavai observed the prime minister for the slightest alteration in his features when he mentioned the Choodamani Vihara. But he gave her no sign of its having any significance.

'Aiya, your mentioning Choodamani Vihara reminds me ... I believe Periya Pazhuvettaraiyar has something against that particular vihara. And it has been exacerbated since the Lankan monks of that order offered the prince the crown and throne of Eezham. Pazhuvettaraiyar might try to cast the blame for the prince going missing on Choodamani Vihara. Would you be so kind as to fortify the vihara with extra security?'

'Right away, amma. I will even send a small army carrying orders from the emperor to Choodamani

Vihara. What are your thoughts on sending Vandiyadevan to Kanchi?'

'Aiya! Is it perhaps not wiser to send someone else on such a discreet mission?'

'If you trust him, I would like to send him. I'm aware of his feats of bravery too. The man we send on this mission must be an asahaya sooran, a man who can fight multiple enemies on his own, who knows no fear. I saw with my own eyes as I entered the palace just how he launched himself at the physician's son. If I hadn't intervened, he'd have been serving as Yama's personal physician by this time!'

Ilaiya Piraatti had to struggle to hide her joy. Yet, she asked with some hesitation, 'But being brave is not quite enough, is it? He is impulsive. He cannot resist a fight.'

'I will send my shishya Tirumalai along. He is the epitome of considered thought and deliberated action,' Aniruddhar said.

Ilaiya Piraatti wondered whether even the gods could read Aniruddha Brahmarayar's mind. So, he was going to send a spy as company for a spy, she thought.

7

A NEW VANATHI

As Kundavai was leaving to ensure Vandiyadevan was freed from prison so that she could send him on his next mission, Vanathi appeared before her and bowed.

'Kanne! I had to leave your side. There are a couple of things I need to do right away. The moment I've finished, I'll be with you. Why don't you go to the garden for a while? Just don't go near the lake!'

'Akka, I won't trouble you any longer. I would like to return to Kodumbalur. Please give me permission,' Vanathi said.

'What, must you join everyone else in burdening me? Why are you angry with me? And what is this newfound love for your birthplace?'

'If I were to be angry with you over anything at all, I would be the worst ingrate who ever lived. And there is no newfound love for my birthplace either. What significance does a birthplace have when the two people who birthed one are dead? I believe my mother had once prayed at the Kali temple near Kodumbalur and promised that she would do a puja there. She passed away before she could fulfil that promise. I faint often, don't I? Perhaps this is because she failed to do the puja.'

'You don't have to travel all the way for the puja. I'll send word and have it done at the Kali temple near Kodumbalur.'

'But it's not just that. My uncle is on his way back from Lanka. He will not come to Pazhaiyarai. Chances are that he will stay back in Thanjavur. I would like to be in Kodumbalur to receive him. I want to ask him in person what exactly transpired in Lanka.'

'Why are you so keen to know what transpired in Lanka?'

'What a question! Have you forgotten that it was in a war in Lanka that my father was martyred?'

'I haven't. But that chapter is closed.'

'I don't think so. My uncle is returning in a hurry before the war is over.'

'So are you going to command him to resume the war in Lanka? Is that why you want to return to Kodumbalur?'

'What right do I have to make such decisions? All I want to know is what happened to prompt his unforeseen return.'

'Ah, I see. You wish to ask your uncle about the heroic deeds Ponniyin Selvan wrought in the war.'

'Would that be wrong, Akka?'

'No, not at all. But it would be wrong for you to abandon me at this time.'

'Akka! I'm not abandoning you, am I? You are surrounded by your other companions, by people who are waiting for your opinions and commands and ...'

'You too, Vanathi? You, too, have begun to talk like everyone else, have you? The news about my brother has affected your mind so badly you're not able to think. Please, don't worry too much about what is being said.'

'How could I be more worried about him than you are, Akka?'

'Tell me the truth. Was it your intention to jump into the lake, or did you genuinely faint?'

'Why would I jump into the water intentionally? I fainted. You and the Vaanar warrior saved me.'

'But you seem to have little gratitude.'

'I will be grateful not only in this birth but in all the seven births accorded to me.'

'You speak as if this birth is over and done with. Listen to me, Vanathi. Stop taxing yourself with worry. I'm sure Arulmozhi Varman is unharmed. I repeat what I told the people of the city at the palace courtyard. Kaveri Amman once saved my bother. It is now Samudra Raja's turn. We will have good news soon.'

'How are you so certain of it, Akka? What evidence do you have that he is safe?'

'An inner voice tells me he is safe. If something had happened to my beloved brother, I would simply know. I would not be able to speak, or walk, or even think. My mind, my heart, my soul, my body would know.'

'I don't trust inner voices, Akka. I have no faith in anything, not in my heart or anyone else's.'

'Why do you say this?'

'For some time now, I've been hallucinating and dreaming and conjuring a particular vision.'

'What vision is that?'

'I see your brother's face in the water. It calls for me. I dream of this image often.'

'But why do you call it a hallucination? It is in line with the news we have received.'

'Once you hear the whole story, you'll realise just what an insane hallucination it is. I fell into the lake in a faint, didn't I? I went to Nagalokam. There was a wedding procession there.'

'Who was getting married?'

'I don't wish to speak of that, Akka. I have no faith in my thoughts, my dreams, even the beliefs I held. I've decided I can only trust what I see with my own eyes and hear with my own ears.'

'Vanathi, you're wrong. We can see and hear things that are not quite real or true. It is our hearts that see the truth. I can think of numerous examples from our epics and folklore that show ...'

'I'll listen to that some other time, Akka. Please give me permission to leave.'

Kundavai was shocked. Where had Vanathi acquired this sudden courage, temerity even? Why, Vanathi had practically cut her off while she was speaking.

'Vanathi, why are you in such a hurry? Even if you must absolutely go to Kodumbalur, can't you leave after a few days? The empire is in turmoil right now. I must ensure that you are well-protected on your journey.'

'I have nothing to fear, Akka. The palanquin bearers and four bodyguards who escorted me from Kodumbalur have been lazing about all these years. They will escort me back now.'

'What an idea! Do you really think I will let you go like that?'

'I beg of you, Akka. I have nothing to fear. No one in this empire would dare harm Kodumbalur Vanathi. Who would invite the wrath of Boothi Vikrama Kesari? Besides, who does not know that I am Ilaiya Piraatti's dearest friend? I ask your permission for just one more thing. I would like to visit the astrologer in Kudandai and ask him a few things. Will you allow me to do so?'

'I would like to consult him too. But you're in such a hurry.'

'No, Akka, this time, I wish to consult him in private.'

Kundavai was speechless from surprise. How had this girl turned so adamant overnight? Not even overnight, in the space of a few hours? She realised there was no way she could stop Vanathi from leaving.

'All right, Vanathi. You have my permission to do as you wish. Go ahead and make arrangements for your journey. I'll release our hero from the prison, and then come to you,' Kundavai said.

8

TWO PRISONS

Once she had given Vanathi permission to return to Kodumbalur, Kundavai Devi made her way straight to the Pazhaiyarai prison. She bade her guards remain outside and went alone to the cell where Vandiyadevan was being held. He was sitting alone, staring at the roof of the cell as he sang a themmangu.[1]

Vaana sudargal ellaam
Mane undanaikandu
Meni silirkudadi
Meimarandu nirkudadi

When the stars in the sky
Gaze upon you, my gazelle
They freeze in awe, and stare
Forgetting even to twinkle

It was only when Kundavai cleared her throat that he turned.

He jumped to his feet and said, 'Welcome, Princess, welcome! Please do be seated!'

'Which seat do I take?' the princess asked.

'This is your palace. Please feel at home. We're bound to your command. You may choose any throne you like in my humble abode,' Vandiyadevan said.

'Aiya, when your ancestors ruled the three worlds, the palace of the Vaanar clan must have looked like this, I presume. Where I come from, they call this a prison cell,' the princess said.

'Ammani, where I come from, there is neither palace nor prison. It has been a hundred years since our enemies banded together to turn them all to dust.'

'Why, why? What irked them so much about your palaces and prisons?'

'It was all because of a poet.'

'Really? Do tell!'

'When my ancestors ruled the southern regions, the tax officials would imprison suzerain kings who defaulted on their tithes. There were prisons for kings right outside the royal palace, arranged around the courtyard. The imprisoned kings would be waiting desperately for the emperor to take pity on them and send for them, so they could beg forgiveness and return home. But it wasn't easy for them to meet the emperor. They would watch as poets and bards were ushered into the royal chambers, where they would recite their poems or sing their songs for the emperor, and return with royal gifts. The kings would be stunned by the rewards these men were given. And then, they began to recognise those gifts. "Oho! Isn't that my regal umbrella?" one king would say. "Adade! This composer is being carried on my palanquin!" another would cry. "Aiyo! He is riding off on my royal elephant!" another would wail. "But that is my horse! My horse will throw this songster off one day or another!" another would say with glee. The poet who brought up the end of the procession heard the suzerain kings' comments and laments, and recited the following poem when it was his turn to meet the emperor:

> *En kavigai en sivigai*
> *En kavas am en thuvasam*
> *En kari yeedhu en pari yeedhu*
> *Enbare; mankavana*
> *Mahavendan vaanan*
> *Varisai parisu petra*
> *Paavendarai vendar paarththu!*
>
> *My umbrella! My palanquin!*
> *My armour! My flag!*
> *My elephant! My horse!*
> *They said; as the kings looked upon*
> *A procession of poets*
> *Blessed by the generosity of*
> *The great king, the Vaanan.*[2]

'This song became hugely popular across Tamizhagam. People would sing it and laugh. And this angered the suzerain kings so much that they got together and marched on us from every side. And they destroyed everything, from our towns to our palaces to our prisons.'

'They destroyed everything but the poem itself, it appears? Your clan must be blessed, for its praises to be sung even today and its good name and reputation to survive against all odds!'

'Well, I believe the responsibility for destroying the reputation and good name of my clan rests solely on my shoulders.'

'Aha! So you accept this truth!'

'I don't have a choice, do I? Of all forms of slavery, the worst is enslavement to a woman. It so happened that I bound myself to a woman's word and had to run and hide and scheme and lie to survive. I was hoping to vent my anger by killing that physician's son, but alas, that mission was interrupted too.'

'Aiya! Why are you so angry with the physician's son Pinagapani?'

'I have reason enough to be angry with him. What a companion you found for my journey to Kodikkarai! He nearly ruined my mission before it began! As if that wasn't enough, he yelled on the streets that I was spying for our enemies and tried to have me captured by the Pazhuvettaraiyar brothers' men. It took my all to escape from that, only for him to declare before the entire town that I was the Pazhuvoor Rani's spy!'

'O Vaanar prince! Is that not true?'

'Is what not true?'

'I'm asking about Pinagapani's charge that you are the Pazhuvoor Rani's spy. Will you tell me the truth?'

'I have taken an oath never to tell the truth, Devi!'

'Aha! What an oath! Was it prompted by your encounter with the Pazhuvoor Rani by the Arichandra River?'

'No, no, I made the decision before that encounter. For as long as I was lying, people believed every word I spoke. Once, I accidentally said, "The prince is safe in Nagapattinam." No one was willing to believe this truth. They all laughed at me.'

'What a terrible thing to do! It's a good thing no one believed you. If they had, what a mess we'd have been in!'

'Such a mistake will never occur again.'

'Thank you very much for giving me your word.'

'My word that ...?'

'That you will carry out the future missions I assign you without such a mistake ever occurring.'

'Kadavule! I have said no such thing. Enough! Please release me from prison, and let me go on my way.'

'Well, in that case, you will not be released. You'll have to remain in prison.'

Vandiyadevan roared with laughter.

'Why do you laugh? Does what I say seem funny to you?'

'No, Devi! If you won't release me from this prison, you think I can't escape?'

With a piercing stare at Vandiyadevan, the princess said, 'Aiya, you're a skilled soldier. And particularly skilled at escaping from prisons. Why, this could barely pose a challenge to a man who could escape from the Pazhuvoor subterranean treasury!'

'In that case, why don't you do the honours and open the door for me?'

'Well, I could release you from this prison. Or you could escape yourself. But there is another prison from which you cannot so much as *dream* of escape.'

'Are you referring to Chinna Pazhuvetta-raiyar's dungeon?'

'No. That would pose no challenge for you either. You could even defeat the hungry tigers in the dungeon.'

'In that case, to which prison do you refer?'

'The prison that is my heart.'

'Devi! I am an orphan. I have no home or hearth to offer you. The pride and prestige of my clan is only remembered in song, perhaps even imagined. You, on the other hand, are the daughter of the emperor who rules the three worlds and ...'

'Who cares? The pride and prestige of the Chozha clan too might one day be remembered only in song.'

'Even so, today you are the undisputed authority of the land. The emperor, the Pazhuvettaraiyar brothers, the prime minister ... none of them would dare flout your wishes.'

'If all this is true, how can you alone flout my wishes?'

'What governs the land is one thing, and what governs the heart is another.'

'And what is wrong with the wishes of my heart?'

'The difference in our social status.'

'Have you not heard the saying *Anbirkum undo adaikkum thaazh?*[3]'

'Well, would that saying not apply to Ponniyin Selvar and Poonguzhali?'

'It would. I believed my brother was born to rule the world. And so, I sought to lock their hearts away from each other.'

'I believed he was born to rule the world too. I was driven by enthusiasm from all that I had heard about the prince. I wanted to accompany him to every corner of the world on his missions of conquest.'

'And that enthusiasm has faded now, hasn't it?'

'Yes. Ponniyin Selvar prefers a quiet life to royal authority. He is keener to dedicate himself to decorating temples than brandishing his sword on the battlefield.'

'And Madurantakan, for his part, is intent on ruling the empire. The goat has turned into a tiger, the tiger into a goat. You know that folktale about how the Aalavaai Iraivan turned a fox into a horse and a horse into a fox[4] and ...'

'Devi, thanks to you, I turned into a fox myself. I ran and hid, schemed and conspired, told lies and spread rumours, all to escape from the enemy! Princess, I can no longer do this work. Please give me leave to go on my way.'

'Aiyo! My dearest friend Vanathi is about to abandon me. Are you going to do that too?'

'Devi! I don't know about the Kodumbalur princess, but how could I possibly abandon you? There are kings and emperors lining up for your hand. Whereas I ... I'm essentially an errand boy ...'

At that moment, Ilaiya Piraatti held out her hand. Vandiyadevan, not sure whether this was a dream or reality, held her delicate hand in both of his and touched her palm to his eyes in a gesture of devotion. His heart and body felt as if they were on fire.

'O Vaanar hero! I was born into a lineage which considers chastity the greatest treasure of its clan. There are women in my family who have walked into their husbands' pyres and burned with them, sitting as calmly as if they were in cool moonlight.'

'I have heard of this, Devi.'

'These hands that have held yours will never hold another man's.'

Vandiyadeven lost his powers of speech and action, and as he looked into Kundavai's brimming eyes, he lost his senses too.

'Aiya! Next time you jump into something, think about what would become of me if there were to be some danger to your life because of your impulsiveness.'

'Devi! Can a man who has been so fortunate as to win a place in your heart be a coward who fears for his life?'

'Cowardice and caution are not the same thing, aiya. The prime minister Aniruddhar himself has no doubt about your courage.'

'Then, what does he doubt?'

'Your fidelity. He suspects you might be the spy of the Pazhuvoor Rani.'

'In that case, I'm happy to respond to him as I did to Pinagapani. Open the door, and tell me where that man is!'

'Pinagapani has had a spot of training in combat, at least. Aniruddhar can only wage war with words, not with swords. His brain is sharper than any blade in the armoury, but he has not so much as touched the edge of a sword.'

'Ah, so mine will have the honour of being the first he touches.'

'Aiya! There is no greater authority in this land than Aniruddha Brahmarayar after the emperor. Even the Pazhuvettaraiyar brothers hesitate to go against him.'

'Their fear is due to their guilt. My conscience is clear. What do I have to fear?'

'He has been a dear friend of my father's since their youth. To disrespect him would be to disrespect both the emperor and me.'

'In that case, tell me how I might win his trust.'

'The prime minister wishes to send a trustworthy man to Kanchi. I have promised him that you would be the best candidate.'

'Devi! Don't send me to Kanchi. There's a voice in my head warning me against going to Kanchi.'

'Perhaps that is the Pazhuvoor Ilaiya Rani's voice?'

'No, not at all. Would I allow that venomous snake's voice to outshout yours?'

'Aiya! Don't ever speak of the Pazhuvoor Rani like that again.'

'What is this I hear? What a change to have come over you!'

'Yes, I have had a complete change of heart where she is concerned. After I heard your news from Lanka.'

'So, from now on, I'll have to treat her with devotion?'

'Yes!'

'If she were to take the deathly sword *she* treats with such devotion, hand it to me and command me to bring back someone's head, I must oblige?'

Kundavai began to tremble. There was a tremor in her voice as she responded.

'You must treat the Pazhuvoor Rani with respect, but you need not obey her every word. She is perhaps unaware of what she is doing?'

'That is exactly what she said too. She said, "I don't know why I'm worshipping this sword with such devotion."'

Kundavai said in an even shakier voice, 'Only God can save this ancient Chozha clan!'

'And may that God use this servant as a tool to save the clan!' Vandiyadevan said.

'Aiya, that is my hope too. Once you return from Kanchi, you must journey to Lanka again. You must, somehow or the other, bring that oomai thaai[5] here.'

'You might as well ask me to bring the tempest back in a pot. Someone made this comparison ... yes, that Veera Vaishnavan! Perhaps he's brought her back himself.'

'No, he wasn't able to. It is you who must.'

'In that case, please don't send me to Kanchi, Devi.'

'Why?'

'Because my master is there. If he asks me to tell him what transpired, I will have to tell him all. The moment he hears the Pazhuvettaraiyar brothers are hatching a conspiracy, he will jump up at once. The moment he hears they are holding the emperor as if he were a prisoner, he will march towards Thanjavur. In fact, if news of Ponniyin Selvar has reached him, he has likely left already.'

'This is exactly why I want to send you and you alone. You must ensure he remains in Kanchi.'

'But what if he leaves before I reach?'

'Then, join him wherever he is. Most important of all, there's one thing you absolutely must do, whatever else you do or don't.'

'Tell me.'

'I hear that Periya Pazhuvettaraiyar has left for the Kadambur palace with the Ilaiya Rani …'

'Is it really the Ilaiya Rani? Or is her palanquin carrying …'

'No, it is certainly her. My uncle is still here.'

'Why is she going?'

'They have invited Aditya Karikalan to Kadambur too. It is ostensibly to bring a proposal of marriage to him. But there is talk that they intend to split the empire in two.'

'My master will never agree to such a thing.'

'That is not what I'm worried about.'

'Then what are you worried about, Devi?'

'I feel a sense of foreboding. My heart is beating fast. "Dhik-dhik", it goes. When I'm half-asleep, I see all sorts of terrible images. When I fall asleep, I have horrible dreams. I wake up trembling and I cannot stop shaking for a long time after.'

'How can I leave your side when you're in such a state? If any peril were to approach you, I would give up my life to …'

'Aiya! I fear not for myself but for my elder brother. I fear the influence that the Pazhuvoor Rani wields where he is concerned. The idea of what might happen if they were to meet makes me quake. You must somehow make sure they don't meet in private.'

'Devi! Who can stop Aditya Karikalar once he makes up his mind about anything?'

'Aiya! You must serve as the armour that protects my brother from injury. If needed, you must tell my brother who Nandini is.'

'But what if he doesn't believe me?'

'It is your duty to say it so that he has no choice but to believe you. I don't know how you will accomplish this. But they must not meet.'

'Devi, I'll do my best. But if I fail, please don't hold it against me.'

'Aiya! Whether you fail or succeed, you will never find release from this prison in which I have enshrined you,' Kundavai Devi said, a hand on her heart.

9

A LADY IN GREEN SILK

The next morning, Vandiyadevan found himself riding at a leisurely pace towards Kudandai, along the banks of the Arisilaru, carrying the scroll Aniruddha Brahmarayar had given him. It was a pleasant time of year, the beginning of the month of Aippasi[1], when the lushness of Chozha Naadu was at its peak. Nature was a queen dressed in green silk, sparkling with youthful beauty.

And what shades of green her finery boasted! The rice crops on the verge of sprouting in the fields were one shade of green, while the saplings that had been planted recently were another; the new sprouts were golden with a tinge of green. The leaves of the banyan tree were one shade of green, and those of the peepal tree another. The luscious leaves of the lotuses that blossomed in the ponds were an enchanting emerald colour, and those of the banana trees yet another shade of green. The ivory green of the coconut palms, the jade green of the water in the ponds, the many shades of the blades of grass that swayed in the wind, and the green of the frogs that jumped from leaf to leaf all gave Vandiyadevan a sense of peace and well-being.

As if to accentuate these various shades, Nature had ornamented herself with kuvalai and kumudam flowers, and lotuses and lilies too.

Vandiyadevan had come the same way during the month of Aadi. How different the landscape looked now! How the waters had bubbled and frothed back then, the same waters that were gently lapping the banks now. He took in ponds that could have passed for slabs of marble, remembering what a roar he had heard then as the river had gushed along, the wind blowing leaves off their branches as it tried to keep up with the water. Now, the leaves rustled in the pleasant breeze, birds twittered and chirped, while toads croaked in expectation of rainfall. The buzzing of the bees through all this left him with a strange sense of melancholy.

It echoed the sadness within him. Why was he sad? He could not tell. He had every reason to be jumping with joy. Every wish and hope he had nursed when he had galloped along this path two months earlier had been realised. Events of which he hadn't dare dream had actually transpired. He had met the emperor Sundara Chozhar; he had been to Thanjavur, Pazhaiyarai, Mathottam and Anuradhapuram, and seen the beauty and grandeur of those ancient cities. He had not only met but also befriended the beloved prince of the people, Ponniyin Selvar. He had even been so lucky as to have played a part in saving his life.

More than anything else, Kundavai Devi—whom one must be blessed to meet in person—had told him she had enshrined him in her heart. His heart thumped with pride and joy when he thought back to those words. And yet, there was a constant underlay of sadness. Perhaps he did not think he truly deserved such luck. Or perhaps he did not believe it would last. There was many a slip between the cup and the lip, and he could lose everything. Kundavai had sworn herself to him, but who knew what obstacles might come in their way?

The world did not lack for obstacles, after all. Mantravadis like Ravidasan, mayamohinis like Nandini, conspirators like the Pazhuvettaraiyar brothers, betrayers like Kandamaaran and Parthibendran, lunatic women like Vanathi and Poonguzhali, spies like the Veera Vaishnava, Kalamukha Shaivites, kolli vaai pisaasus, quicksand pits ... the world was full of those, wasn't it? God had been kind enough to save him from every one of these thus far. Only for Aniruddha Brahmarayar to pitch him into the greatest peril of all. On the one hand, he would have to deal with Aditya Karikalan, who barely needed provocation to fly into blind rages and make rash decisions. On the other, there was Nandini who had contrived to make puppets out of such warriors as the Pazhuvettaraiyar brothers.

And he had been assigned to figure out what her intentions were, and nip her plans in the bud. What an impossible task! What was the prime minister's real motive, he wondered. What if sending him on a fool's errand was a ruse to separate him from the princess?

The princess and prime minister had said Azhvarkadiyaan would be joining him, but there was no sign of the Vaishnavite yet. Whatever his faults were, Azhvarkadiyaan hadn't caused Vandiyadevan any harm thus far. He had, in fact, got him out of a scrape or two. The journey would be less arduous with him around. He would chatter non-stop, and keep Vandiyadevan in good spirits. But how long could he keep the horse dawdling in the hope that Azhvarkadiyaan would join him? Perhaps the Vaishnavite had other plans, he thought.

Ah! There was the tree with its thick, gnarled roots peeping out of the water and looking like crocodiles. This was the spot where his own adventure with the dummy crocodile had played out. How Varini and Tarakai and Sendiru and Mandakini had laughed at him, only for the princess to tell them off and apologise to him on their behalf! This would be a good spot to rest for a while, Vandiyadevan thought.

He got off his horse and stood by the riverbank. He looked at the clear water winding its way past stones and sand, and thought he saw a face in it. Whose face was it? Ah! It was the lovely face of the princess, Kundavai Devi.

Kanden kanden kanden
Kannukiniyana kanden!

I saw, I saw, I saw,
I saw sweet sights!

The voice made Vandiyadevan turn with a start. He saw Azhvarkadiyaan perched on one of the higher branches of a tall tree.

'Oho! So I'm such a sweet sight to your precious eyes, am I? Do come down so I can get a good look at you and return the compliment,' Vandiyadevan called to him.

'I wasn't talking about you, appane!' Azhvarkadiyaan retorted, as he slithered down the tree. 'With your sword and spear, you're more scary than sweet!'

'Then whom were you speaking of?'

'When the greatest of gods Vishnu took the Vamana avataram and lifted one foot to claim the skies, your Shiva Peruman ...'

'Enough, Vaishnavare! Stop belittling Shiva Peruman now. Or you'll be subject to great peril!'

'What peril, appane? Why must I fear any peril when the Sudarshana chakra of Vishnu is waiting to protect me, as it protected Gajendra from a crocodile?'

'I've said what I have to say. The rest is up to you.'

'Do tell me what peril I might be subject to, thambi!'

'When the people of Pazhaiyarai mobbed the palace, I heard some of the Kalamukhas speaking to each other.'

'What did they say?'

'They said they should round up all the Veera Vaishnavites in Chozha Naadu, whose numbers have spiked of late, offer them as sacrifices to Mahakali and arrange their skulls to make a platform, on which they would dance the Ananda Tandavam!'

Azhvarkadiyaan felt the top of his head and said, 'Hmm. My skull is solid. I'm sure it will bear the weight of the Ananda Tandavam.'

'I saw them all along the way I came, Kalamukhas striding along, each with a skull in one hand and trishul in another. You're best off giving up this topknot of yours and adopting their hairdo and saying "Shivane", so that ...'

'Oh, no, no, impossible!'

'What's impossible?'

'I cannot speak that name you said. I could change my appearance, as long as I can shout "Vishnuve", maybe ... oh, look!'

A palanquin was being carried along the riverbank. They could see a woman seated inside, but they could not see her face. Who was it? She must be a royal of some sort, but from where? She was accompanied by a maid, and had no other escort. The only others in the party were the palanquin bearers. Could it be Princess Kundavai? No, surely not!

'Vaishnavare! Do you know who is in the palanquin?' Vandiyadevan asked.

'Thambi! Listen to me. Don't poke your nose into things that don't concern you and get caught up in other people's business! Haven't you got into enough scrapes because of this propensity of yours? You will encounter numerous passers-by on your journey. Why does it matter to you who they are, or what they want? Get on your horse and spur him on, go!'

'Oho, so our Veera Vaishnavar has turned into a philosopher, has he? Have you forgotten what happened in Veeranarayanapuram? Didn't you ask me to carry a message to the occupant of a closed palanquin?'

'Why are you dragging out those old stories now?'

'Well, I'll let it go. They said you'd be accompanying me on the journey. I was dawdling my horse along to give you a chance to join me. Now, are you coming with me or not?'

'You'll be on your horse, and I on foot. How, then, can we go together? Go wait at the banks of the Kollidam. I'll join you there tomorrow morning.'

Vandiyadevan was now certain that Azhvarkadiyaan was on some other secret mission and would not be joining him.

'Well, as you wish!' he said, and got on the horse. He looked in the direction he was to go, and then studied the sky. He saw clouds gathering in the northeasterly direction.

'Vaishnavare! Will it rain tonight?' he asked.

'Appane! Have I ever claimed to be an astrologer? It is the month of Aippasi. There's a fair chance of rainfall. It would be prudent for you to hurry along and make sure you find a resting place for the night,' Azhvarkadiyaan said.

Vandiyadevan spurred his horse on.

Have I ever claimed to be an astrologer?

The Vaishnavite's words stayed with him. They reminded him of the astrologer he had met at Kudandai. The astrologer's house was on the way. Why not stop to see him, Vandiyadevan thought. Which of the aspirants to the Chozha throne would succeed? The astrologer had compared Ponniyin Selvar to the Dhruva nakshatram. And here was Ponniyin Selvar saying he had no interest in ruling a kingdom. He hadn't hesitated a moment in refusing the bejewelled crown and royal throne of Lanka when they were offered to him. The astrologer had said there were various dangers approaching the prince, and that he would be subject to trials and tribulations. This prediction was already coming true. Would the grand future the astrologer had envisioned for the prince come true as well?

And what about Vandiyadevan himself? Would his dreams come true? Would the empire his ancestors had lost ever be regained? And how successful would his current mission be? Could he possibly stand between Aditya Karikalar and Nandini, and prevent whatever disaster was approaching? He had escaped from Nandini every time he had met her. But would that happen this time? Vandiyadevan was discomfited by the thought of the Pazhuvoor Ilaiya Rani. She had shown him nothing but kindness and respect, even fondness. But he wasn't able to read her mind or look into her heart. He had a sense that she had spared him for some important reason, that she intended to put him to some use in the future. But what could the reason be, and how could he be of use to her?

Vandiyadevan's horse now went past the palanquin that he had seen a short while earlier. He had no intention of running into *this* palanquin. Neither did the party inside wish to have anything to do with him. Yet, as he passed by the palanquin, its curtains parted in the breeze and he couldn't help looking inside. He recognised the princess of Kodumbalur. He wondered whether he should stop and speak to her. Then, he decided against it.

He was reminded of what Kundavai had said about Vanathi. Why was the princess setting off all by herself at such a turbulent time, without even an adequate escort? Suddenly, he noticed two Kalamukha Shaivites in the distance, squinting intently at the palanquin. Why were they staring at it like that? Who were they? Weren't they the same Kalamukhas who had passed by him when he had been pretending to sleep earlier?

It was true that Vandiyadevan wasn't overly fond of Vanathi. He felt she was trying to snatch the place in Ponniyin Selvar's heart that was Poonguzhali's by right. And this made him feel hostile towards her. Yet, he couldn't overlook the fact that Kundavai adored her. If Vanathi were to come to harm, his beloved would not be able to bear it. But why should the Kodumbalur princess come to any harm?

Azhvarkadiyaan's words came to mind:

Don't poke your nose into things that don't concern you and get caught up in other people's business.

Even so, the sight of the Kalamukhas staring at the palanquin had made him uneasy. But ... ah! Here was the house of the Kudandai astrologer. He would speak to him and ask about this too ... adade! Vanathi must be making her way here too, he thought. Well, his problem was solved. She would stop here for a while, and he could deliberate his course of action then. In the meantime, he would finish consulting the astrologer himself.

Vandiyadevan stopped his horse at the threshold of the astrologer's house, dismounted and made his way inside.

10

BRAHMA'S FIFTH HEAD

As Vandiyadevan entered the Kudandai astrologer's house for the second time, his heart was suddenly filled with joy. He realised it was an involuntary somatic reaction to his memory of having set eyes on Kundavai for the first time, in this very house. He had been arrested by her lotus-like face and the large black eyes that had widened in surprise upon seeing him barge in. It was here that he had first heard her lilting voice, sweeter than honey. The memories washed over his heart like waves dancing on a full moon night. His ears, his heart, his entire body quivered with happiness and a sense of fulfilment.

The astrologer was preparing for his evening puja.

'Come, appane, welcome! You are Vandiyadevan Vallavarayan of the Vaanar clan, aren't you?' he said.

'Yes, josiyare! Your predictions might be off, but no one can fault your memory,' Vandiyadevan said.

'Thambi, memory is crucial to learning the shastras that deal with the science of astrology. The planets, stars, ascendants, buddhis, yogas, they can fall into a million different arrangements and alignments. We must remember all these even as we calculate their positions during a particular year, month, day, time, second, a hundredth fraction of a second ... and then make the calculations that govern one's birth chart. Well, that's as may be. You said my predictions were off? What did you mean? Did nothing I had predicted for you come to pass?'

'Can't you tell using your expertise in astrology?'

'Indeed I can. I could use my expertise in astrology, or I could use common sense. My predictions must have come true, or you wouldn't have returned.'

'Yes, yes, your predictions did come true.'

'Oh, there we go! In what ways did they come true?'

'Exactly as you said they would. You said, "Your mission could succeed; or, it might not." And that's exactly what happened. I would be lying if I said it "happened". Because it didn't quite unfold smoothly, you see. Your grand prediction took one look at me and ran for its life.'

'Thambi, you're quite the joker.'

'That's true enough. I *am* a joker. A joker with a temper.'

'You should have packed your temper into a bundle and left it outside my house when you entered.'

'I considered that course of action. But then, I didn't see your shishya outside. What if a passer-by made off with my temper while I was inside? So I decided not to leave it unguarded and brought it inside with me. Where is your shishya, by the way? The memory of his refusing to let me in last time is still fresh.'

'Today is the new moon night of Aippasi. He must have gone to the banks of the Kollidam river.'

'What does the new moon night of Aippasi have to do with the Kollidam river?'

'There is a Maha Sangam of the Kalamukhas tonight by the banks of the Kollidam. My shishya belongs to the Kalamukha sect.'

'Josiyare! I'm contemplating renouncement of Shaivism.'

'Renounce it ...'

'Your friend Azhvarkadiyaan ...'

'Are you referring to Tirumalai?'

'Yes. I'm planning on getting initiated into Vaishnavism by him, to smear myself with the naamam of Vishnu all over my body, and follow his footsteps into Veera Vaishnavism.'

'Why, though?'

'I saw some Kalamukha Shaivites. On my way here, even. The sight of them, with their innovative uses for human skulls, makes me want to renounce Shaivism.'

'Thambi! You're the veteran of several wars. Why should skulls frighten you?'

'They don't frighten me. But they do disgust me. What does killing the enemy on the battlefield have to do with wearing necklaces of skulls?'

'Didn't your master Aditya Karikalan take out a procession around the city brandishing the severed head of Veerapandiyan?'

'He was doing that because of some oath he had sworn. And has been regretting it since. Also, he doesn't wear necklaces made of skulls. And doesn't walk about using them as bowls either. Why do the Kalamukhas do that?'

'So that we don't forget that life is transient. You and I wear vibhuti on our foreheads. How is that different? We do it to remind ourselves that this human body is only a vessel that will one day turn to the very ash we smear on our skin.'

'Sure, mortal bodies are impermanent. They will burn and become ash, or they will rot and turn into dust, but that is not the case with Shiva Peruman, is it? Why does he walk about with skulls for ornaments?'

'Thambi, the skull in Shiva's hand symbolises pride. If one can overcome pride and ego, one will attain Ananda—bliss. Shiva dances the Ananda Tandavam with a skull in hand, no?'

'How does the human skull symbolise pride? I don't see it.'

'There's a lot you don't see. Thambi! For now, let me tell you why the human skull symbolises pride. Once, Brahma and Vishnu got into an argument over which of them was the greater god. Shiva intervened, and said, "One of you go find the top of my head, and the other the tip of my toes. Whoever returns first after having seen his object is the greater god of you." Mahavishnu took on the Varaha avataram and dug into the bowels of the earth to find the feet of Shiva. Brahma took on the form of a swan, and flew high into the sky. Vishnu returned and admitted that he had not been able to find Shiva's feet. Whereas Brahma returned and lied that he had seen Shiva's topknot. Shiva then used two fingers to pinch off Brahma's fifth head as punishment for his lie. It was his pride that had brought about Brahma's predicament. The skull Shiva carries is Brahma's.'

Vandiyadevan nearly fell over laughing.

'What is so funny about this?'

'Nothing, nothing. Something came to mind, that's all.'

'And what might that be? Is it a secret?'

'Not at all. I was just thinking that if I were to be punished as Brahma was, I'd need at least ten thousand spare heads.'

'Is that how many lies you've told?'

'Indeed, josiyare, at the very least. It must be a quirk in my horoscope. After I met Ponniyin Selvar, I decided to stop lying. Then, I told an important truth. Everyone who heard it burst out laughing. No one believed me.'

'Yes, thambi, that is what the world has come to. People barely believe lies these days. What are the chances of their believing the truth?'

'That must be the case with your predictions too. Josiyare! Do you remember what you said about Ponniyin Selvar? You said he was like the Dhruva nakshatram, didn't you? The pole star that remains due north?'

'Yes, I did. What of it?'

'Have you not heard the news about him?'

'How could I not have? People have been talking of nothing else.'

'Have you ever heard of the Dhruva nakshatram drowning at sea?'

'The Dhruva nakshatram will not drown. But even the pole star may be hidden by clouds every now and again. Even today, we see clouds gathering in the northern sky. Try as one might, one will not see the Dhruva nakshatram tonight. Does that mean it is no longer there?'

'Is that how you feel? Have you got any solid news of Ponniyin Selvar, then?'

'How could I? They say you're the one who last saw him, that both of you jumped into the sea together. If anyone should have solid news of him, it is you. I was planning to ask you, in fact.'

Vandiyadevan decided it was time to change the subject, and asked, 'Josiyare, how is the comet doing?'

'Its tail is very long these days. It can't get much longer than this. If Dhoomaketu is to wreak any harm on us, it is likely to occur very soon. Kadavule! Who knows what will befall which royal?' the astrologer sighed.

A series of images flitted through Vandiyadevan's mind—of the bedridden emperor in Thanjavur; of Arulmozhi Varmar shivering with fever in Nagapattinam; of Aditya Karikalar who had been invited to the Kadambur palace to meet Nandini; of Nandini herself, who was coddling a deathly sword.

'Well, all that's as it may be, josiyare. Royal matters don't concern us, do they? Tell me, is my current mission likely to succeed?'

'I can only tell you what I said earlier, appane. You will face numerous obstacles and dangers. And you will always find help from unexpected quarters.'

There was a knock at the door. Vandiyadevan wondered whether it was danger or help that was knocking. They could hear the voices of men and women in the courtyard. Both men turned towards the entrance.

Vanathi and her maid walked into the house.

Vandiyadevan got to his feet and bowed. 'Devi, do forgive me,' he said. 'If only I'd known you were on your way here, I wouldn't have come.'

/ *11*

VANATHI ASKS A FAVOUR

'Aiya, why are you so angry with me? What ill have I done you?' the princess of Kodumbalur asked.

Her frail voice melted Vandiyadevan's heart. What reason did he have to be angry with this girl, really? Poonguzhali's face flashed before him. But how was it fair to dislike Vanathi for her desiring the same man as Poonguzhali?

'Ammani! Do forgive me. I did not mean anything of the sort. I simply meant I would have allowed you to see the astrologer first, and waited outside until you had finished. I'm in no hurry. Even now, actually ...'

'You don't have to leave. I'm glad you're in no hurry. Truth be told, I didn't come here to consult the astrologer. I've lost all faith in his abilities.'

'Devi! I consider it my honour to have elicited an opinion from you, be what it may. One day, you will realise that every single prediction I've made was right, and you will shower praise on me,' the astrologer said.

'We'll see about that at the time,' Vanathi said, and then turned to Vandiyadevan. 'Aiya! I came here to meet you. I saw you pass us by on your horse. I thought you might stop to talk to me, but you went ahead as if you hadn't seen me. But that's no surprise. Why would anyone care about an orphan like me?'

Vandiyadevan was so filled with pity by her words he thought he might well up. 'Devi, why do you speak this way?' he asked. 'The beloved daughter of Kodumbalur Siriya Velaar, the niece and ward of Periya Velaar Boothi Vikrama Kesari, the commander of the southern armies, the dearest friend and confidant of Ilaiya Piraatti cannot be called an "orphan"! I did not stop to talk to you because it would be poor form to stop a lady's entourage and exchange pleasantries en route. That was the only reason I rode ahead. If there's anything I can do for you …'

'Yes, aiya, indeed there is. I came here to ask a huge favour of you.'

'Please tell me. If it is within my capacity …'

'Is there anything at all that is not within your capacity? I've heard about the perils you encountered on your way to Lanka and during your time there. Will you promise to do me the favour I'm about to ask?'

Vandiyadevan said, with some hesitation, 'Devi! It would be best if you told me the nature of the favour you ask.'

'True. I shouldn't trick you into making a promise. Fine, I'll tell you what it is. The astrologer might as well hear it. I intend to convert to Buddhism and become a bhikshuni.'

'What? What did you say?'

'What an idea!'

'Never! Never, ever!'

'The world cannot bear such a thing!'

'It cannot happen!'

Vandiyadevan and the astrologer took turns exclaiming in horror at Vanathi's declaration. Having heard them out patiently, she said, 'Yes, I have decided to become a Buddhist sanyasini. Why do you have so many objections to the idea? What is wrong with my decision? Haven't numerous women in ancient Tamizhagam taken on a life of ascetism? Why, Manimeghalai[1] attained divinity by embracing just such a life. Don't we refer to her as "Manimeghalai Deivam—The Goddess Manimeghalai" even today? I don't nurse such grand ambitions. I tried to end this useless, pointless, unworthy life. I failed. It appears it is God's will that I should live a little longer. I'd like to spend whatever time is ordained to me at a Buddhist monastery, working for humanity, showing compassion to everyone. Surely, you won't hesitate to help me out in this pursuit?'

Vandiyadevan began to feel slightly suspicious.

'Devi,' he said, 'while your decision is not right or fair in any way, it is not my place to voice my opinion. The elders in your family are the ones who must discuss this with you. Your uncle Senapati Boothi Vikrama Kesari is on his way back, and …'

'Aiya, I don't intend to wait for anyone, or discuss this with anyone. I have made my decision. I request a favour from you in this respect.'

'What favour could I possibly do you where this is concerned, devi?'

'I'll tell you. I am heading to the Choodamani Viharam in Nagapattinam, with the intention of requesting the monks there to initiate me into the order by performing a deeksha ceremony. Would you please accompany me there? So I won't be all alone? That is the favour I ask.'

Vandiyadevan jumped out of his skin. The Kodumbalur princess was something else, he thought. She must have heard some part of his exchange with Ilaiya Piraatti. Her intention in making for the Choodamani Viharam was to meet the prince there. Vandiyadevan thought to himself that he could not possibly enable this.

'Ammani! Please forgive me, but I am not empowered to grant your request.'

'What a bizarre thing you say! A man who has worked all sorts of wonders travelling at great peril to Eezham feels it is beyond his powers to escort an orphan to Nagapattinam!'

'Devi, I did not say it was beyond my powers. I meant, I'm not in a position to take it on at this moment. The prime minister and Ilaiya Piraatti have asked me to make my way to Kanchi as soon as possible, with a scroll too. That is why I've had to refuse the favour you ask. If only the circumstances had been different ...'

'Sure, sure. One can think of a million excuses if one wants to avoid something. But that isn't a problem. I started out with the intention of travelling alone. But the groups of Kalamukhas I saw on the way left me feeling apprehensive. Well, but God watches over me, the God who protects all life. I'm passing on the burden of protecting me to Him now! What can anyone do to a woman who is about to renounce the world and take up a life of ascetism? I'll take your leave, aiya. And yours, josiyare!'

Vanathi turned and walked out of the house.

The astrologer ran after her, saying, 'Devi! Devi! It's nearing nightfall. And it is a new moon night too. And clouds have been gathering in the northeast. Can't you stay in my humble home for the night, and leave in the morning?'

'No, josiyare, please excuse me, but I plan to reach Tiruvarur by tonight, and stay there. This man has refused to escort me. But surely, I'll find someone reliable in Tiruvarur? That said, I don't really care too much for my life either. Of what use am I to anyone, anyway?'

Those were the last words Vandiyadevan and the astrologer would hear from her. The next moment, Vanathi mounted the palanquin that was waiting outside. The palanquin went on its way. The two men stared after it until it disappeared from view.

Then, Vandiyadevan said, 'Until recently, the Kodumbalur princess was afraid of her own shadow. Ilaiya Piraatti's other companions used to tease her all the time. They tried scaring her with a fake crocodile. I was the one who got fooled instead. Now, all of a sudden, this woman is brave enough to make such a long journey all by herself. Where did she acquire such courage? And how did Ilaiya Piraatti give her consent to leave?'

'Yes, that surprises me too. The last time this girl visited me, she fainted suddenly. Then, she spoke in a frail voice. I simply can't believe this is the same person. How sharp-tongued she is now! And how daring she sounds!'

'What do you think prompted the change?' Vandiyadevan asked.

'Perhaps she has been sent into shock by some important news she has received.'

'What news could that be?'

'Why, isn't the news of Ponniyin Selvar drowning at sea enough? The word is that this girl is all set to marry the prince.'

Vandiyadevan wondered whether it was the news of Ponniyin Selvar having drowned at sea, or of his having survived and been ensconced in the Choodamani Viharam, or what he had told Ilaiya Piraatti about Poonguzhali and the prince, that had had such an effect on Vanathi.

'But, josiyare, members of the Kodumbalur royal family have traditionally been Veera Shaivites. What could have drawn this girl to Buddhism all of a sudden?' he asked.

'Perhaps it is a connection from an earlier birth,' the astrologer said.

'But why to the Choodamani Viharam at Nagapattinam?'

'I don't understand that either,' the astrologer said.

'Won't your knowledge of astrology help you figure it out?'

'What does astrology have to do with this? It is knowledge of spyology[2] that one must have.'

'Does such a branch of knowledge as "spyology" exist?'

'Why not? Haven't you heard of Poyyaamozhi Pulavar's *Tirukkural*?[3]'

'I remember having heard that there was a work of that name.'

'There is a section titled "Spyology" in that work. It contains ten couplets.'

'Really, tell me one or two of those!'

'They're all quite brilliant. Right, here's one:

Vinaiseivar thanchutram vendaadhaar endraangu
Anaivaraiyum aaraaivadhu otru.

Employees, near and dear ones, enemies——to
Analyse them all is to spy.

'Do you know what this means? A king must have spies to analyse everyone in his employ, his relatives and friends, as well as all his enemies. Then, there's this one:

Thurandaar padivaththa ragi irandhaaraainthu
Enjeyinum sorvila thotru.

Mendicants, ascetics, corpses—to pass for those,
And yet yield to nothing is to spy.

'This means that a good spy should be able to disguise himself as an ascetic or mendicant, stay still as a corpse or even pretend to be one when called for, and not say a word or reveal a thing by deed or expression, no matter how horrifically he is tortured by enemies or captors.

'And that's not all. Valluvar says a king must employ a spy to spy on another:

Otrotri thantha porulaiyum matrumor
Otrinaal otri kolal.

What's learned by nuanced spying must be
Verified by another spy.

'You really haven't heard any of these quoted?'

Vandiyadevan was stunned. The moment he was able to find the time, he must read *Tirukkural* before he did anything else, he decided. A man who had thought so deeply about governance and royal matters, an entire millennium ago, must truly be a genius, he thought.

He chatted for a while with the astrologer and went on his way, turning down the latter's offer to host him for the night.

'I'll come back here, and then I will stay as your guest,' Vandiyadevan said.

'When you do come back here, it will be after you've seen that my predictions have come true,' the astrologer said.

'Aiyo, josiyare! But you have made no predictions! How can they come true unless you've *predicted* them in the first place?' Vandiyadevan said with a laugh, as he jumped on his horse and rode away.

For some distance beyond the astrologer's house, there was only the one road. The palanquin must have gone that way. Later, the road forked into two. One went northwards to the Kollidam river. Another went southeast towards Tiruvarur. Vandiyadevan could make out the palanquin and its retinue far, far away, on the Tiruvarur road. His mind floundered a bit.

He had turned down the Kodumbalur princess's request for an escort to Nagapattinam. What if she really needed help? What if something terrible were to befall her en route? Would he ever forgive himself for it? Wouldn't he forever regret that moment, when he had turned her down? But what choice had he had? The prime minister and Ilaiya Piraatti had sent him on an urgent mission. He couldn't afford to be distracted by other matters. He had suffered enough for intervening in issues that did not concern him. Azhvarkadiyaan had warned him against repeating that mistake. Besides, he oughtn't to so much as dream of escorting anyone to the prince's hideout.

Having arrived at this conclusion, Vandiyadevan guided his horse towards the road that led to Kollidam. Even as he chose the path, he thought he heard a shout, and then a woman's scream, all very faint. Startled, he turned back around, only to find that the palanquin had disappeared from sight. Perhaps it had gone down a bend in the road. Even so, he should make sure. That wouldn't cause much of a delay. Having made up his mind, Vandiyadevan spurred his horse on, and galloped towards the spot where he had last seen the palanquin. The sight he saw there made his heart stop. A woman had been tied to a tree. Her mouth had been stuffed with a cloth so she couldn't shout. He couldn't make out who she was at first, in the dark of the night. When he went closer, he realised she was the maid from Vanathi's retinue. She was making muffled noises as she tried to free herself. Vandiyadevan leapt off the horse and first pulled out the cloth from her mouth, before freeing her from the ropes that bound her. It struck him that they had been tied rather loosely.

'Penne! What happened here! Tell me fast! Where is the palanquin? And your princess?' he asked, in a panic.

The maid fumbled through her response. As the palanquin and its entourage had gone round the bend in the road, a group of five or six men had accosted them by leaping out of hiding spots in the trees. Some of them had been carrying skulls and trishuls. Two of them had hit the maid on the head and pushed her aside. They had stuffed her mouth with cloth even as the rest had surrounded the palanquin. They had threatened the palanquin-bearers, who had then run off the road onto a little footpath, with the palanquin. The group that had waylaid them ran after the palanquin. Through all this, not a peep had been heard from Vanathi. Having said all this, the maid pointed out the footpath to him.

'Penne! Make your way to the astrologer's house and stay there. I will see if I can find the princess,' Vandiyadevan said, and leapt back on his horse, leading the animal off the main road and down the footpath. The horse galloped along, notwithstanding the uneven surface and the undergrowth that interrupted the path every so often.

12

WHEN THE TORCH WENT OUT

It was a new moon night. Darkness reigned everywhere. The clouds that had gathered in the north had now spread across the sky. Not a single star pierced the night sky. The fireflies that gathered around the trees and bushes offered some vestige of light. Vandiyadevan guided his horse with the help of their meagre glow. Where was he going? To what end? Would he be of any use? He had no idea. Kundavai Piraatti's dearest friend was in danger, and it was his duty to try and help. And then, it was God's will.

Even after riding a whole naazhigai, he found no sign of the palanquin. He wondered whether he was doing something completely insane. He pulled his horse to a stop. Just then, he heard a far-off sound. He listened hard, and realised it was the sound of a horse's hooves. Was it a single horse, or several? They could be horsemen escorting a palanquin. He would have to be careful. He didn't want to find himself in the middle of a crowd and then in another scrape. That would render him useless to Vanathi. And he would fail in his mission too.

He treaded as softly as he could with the horse, following the sound of the hooves. He ascertained that it was coming from a single horse. Then, the sound changed, and he thought the horse might be climbing up a slope. Vandiyadevan had to make sure he wasn't spotted. So, he stayed back for a bit and took in his surroundings. There was an old ruin nearby, with broken walls. He went close to the ruin and stopped his horse near a wall. He squinted so hard at the horse he was pursuing that his eyes started to hurt.

'Who goes there?' a voice shouted.

Vandiyadevan was startled by the cry. It was a familiar voice.

'Maharaja! It is I! At your service!' someone else cried.

A torch appeared and moved towards the spot where the horse was. The man carrying it had been hiding among the trees. Vandiyadevan saw that the horse rider was Madurantakan.

As the torch-bearer raised his arm, the sudden flash of fire startled the horse, who reared up, swung round and then took off at a gallop. The horse had been standing on the high bank of a wide canal. Now, the animal jumped into the water.

The man with the torch shouted, 'Maharaja! Maharaja!' as he ran behind the horse.

He followed the horse into the water, and lost his balance. The torch in his hand went out.

Now, the darkness seemed even more impenetrable than before. It began to drizzle too. The swishing of the tree leaves, the pitter-patter of the rain, the croaking of the frogs and the thud of horses' hooves were interspersed with panicked human voices, making for a bizarre cacophony.

Vandiyadevan was aware that horsemanship was not Madurantakan's forte. The prince wasn't known for his courage either. What would the poor man come to, riding a horse that had been scared into a gallop? The horse might have done anything to him— he might well have been thrown off right away; or the horse might have carried him into the water; or, if he was still in the saddle, he was likely to be thrown off at some point.

Would the man who had been carrying the torch pursue the horse successfully and save Madurantakan? But he himself had slipped in the water! The man would have to save himself before thinking about the prince.

Vandiyadevan then wondered what he should do now. Go in search of Vanathi? Or rush to Madurantakan's aid?

He had no clue which way Vanathi Devi had gone. But Madurantakan had been carried away on a terrified horse right before his eyes. It would be easy to find him and help him. Once he had made sure Madurantakan was all right, Vandiyadevan could resume his search for Vanathi. Kadavule! He had only just made up his mind not to intervene in matters that were of no concern to him, and now here he was, trying to choose between two such matters!

He went to fetch his own horse. Relying on his instincts, he made his way through the darkness and drizzle to the spot where he had seen Prince Madurantakan's horse plunge into the water. He led his horse into the canal, and then took a look around.

He couldn't see much, but he could hear inarticulate sounds from a distance—'aaaa', 'eeee', 'oooo', 'dadapada-dadapada', 'kadakada-kadakada'!

He crossed the canal and rode up the opposite bank. He squinted into the distance again. All he could see were paddy fields ahead of him. He would not be able to navigate past the stagnant water and young crops on horseback. His only option was to ride along the bank and go searching.

But the bank was overgrown with thorns, nettles and bushes. He discerned a footpath through all the underbrush, and guided his horse carefully. It was raining hard now, and the ground was slushy. The canal was on one side, and paddy fields on the other. Thorns were everywhere. His horse moved slowly. Every moment seemed like an age. As the drizzle turned into a torrent from above, the darkness intensified.

Vandiyadevan's head was crowded with thoughts and questions.

Why was Madurantaka Devar travelling alone on horseback? Where was he headed? Who was the man who had been waiting for him? Were the two incidents of the evening—Madurantakan's journey and Vanathi's kidnapping—somehow related? What would have become of Vanathi by now? And why had he himself contrived to get caught up in all this? Why was he pursuing this now, instead of going about the task he had been assigned? Then again, how could he possibly rush forward in the rain? And, also, how could he decide that these events were not his concern?

The midnight conference at Kadambur Sambuvarayar's palace had nothing to do with him, and yet spying on it had proven immensely useful. But this pathetic journey along the river in sheets of rain and through mud and slush could not possibly be of any use. The only outcome would be getting soaked to the bone. And if the horse tripped and fell, and ended up breaking a leg or two ... no! He couldn't afford to take such a risk.

His best bet was to return to the ruin, and wait out the rain.

Just then, a flash of lightning lit up the entire landscape and Vandiyadevan thought he saw a horse standing at an elevation in the distance. Well, he had already come all this way. He might as well go a little longer, and see what had become of Madurantakan. Who knew how helpful it might be to become the hero of the evening, save Madurantakan's life and win his gratitude forever?

He led his own horse towards Madurantakan's. The mound on which the horse had been standing appeared to be at a considerable height. There was another flash of lightning, and he saw that there was no rider on the horse. There was a clap of thunder, which frightened the horse into a run. There was little point in pursuing the animal now.

Madurantakan might be lying somewhere, having been thrown off the horse.

Vandiyadevan began to call in a stentorian voice that pierced through the 'rim-rim', 'jhim-jhim' of the rain, 'Who goes there?' His voice bounced off the hills and rocks and came back to him in an echo from every direction ... 'Who goes there?' 'Who goes there?' 'Who goes there?'

As the rain had turned into a torrent, the wind had become a gale. Its force turned the raindrops horizontal and they pierced Vandiyadevan in the face. His horse stopped to shake himself every now and again. The cold and rain had got to Vandiyadevan too. He shivered and his teeth chattered.

There was no point in dallying anymore. Vandiyadevan turned his horse around. As he made his way to the ruin, he regretted his foolishness. He should not have delayed his journey by poking his nose into anything else. He should have simply looked to himself and his mission.

The horse's instincts guided them to the ruin. The animal neighed upon arrival, and this brought Vandiyadevan back to the real world. He got off his mount. His clothes were soaked. He would have to spread them out to dry. He decided to explore the ruin and see if he could find a covered spot for himself and the horse.

Now imagine, you're in open space, in pouring rain, when someone lights a fire under your feet ... how you would jump! That's exactly how Vandiyadevan jumped. And the reason was ... not a ghost or ghoul, but the voice of a little child.

'Amma! Amma!'

Then again, how could he be so sure it wasn't a ghost or ghoul? How could a child's voice find its way into this ruin at this time? Who was to say it wasn't a ghost speaking in the voice of a child? No, no! There was no such thing. Chhi, chhi! Ghosts and ghouls were born from the imagination of cowards in moments of terror.

'Amma! Amma! Whaaan ... humm, humm ... whaaan ... humm, humm ...'

No, this was certainly the voice of a human child. A frightened child, whimpering from fear, separated from his mother!

The voice came from the darkest corner of the ruin. Was the child all alone? Was there no accompanying adult?

'Amma! Amma! ... humm, humm ... humm, humm ...'

Vandiyadevan approached the spot from which the voice came and called, 'Who goes there?'

The child's voice came right back: 'Who goes there?'

'It is I? Who are you? What are you doing in the dark? Come on out!'

'But it's raining out!'

'The rain has stopped. Come!'

'Where is my Amma?'

'Your Amma has gone to buy you milk.'

'No! You're lying!'

'Will you come on out, or shall I come in?'

'Enter at your peril! I have a knife with me. I'll kill you.'

'Ade appa! You seem to be a great warrior! Come on out and kill me.'

'Who are you? Not a tiger, are you?'

'Not a tiger, I'm a horse,' Vandiyadevan said.

'Liar! Can a horse talk?'

'Can a tiger talk, then?'

'Amma said there are tigers about, and if I come out of this spot, they might pounce on me.'

'I'm not a tiger. And I don't intend to pounce on you either. You may come out without fear.'

'Fear? I'm not afraid!' said the voice indignantly, even as a tiny child—little more than an infant— toddled out of the ruin.

The rain had let up completely by this time. The clouds had parted, and starlight shone down on them. Vandiyadevan studied the child. He was probably about four years old. And had a proud, handsome face already. He wore a little silk cloth around his waist, and a ratnamala around his neck.

The child must be from an aristocratic family. Who was the mother who had left him all by himself? And why had she come here? Why had she gone away?

The child, too, had been assessing Vandiyadevan. He looked him up and down and said, 'You're not a horse. You look like a man to me.'

'Look, there's a horse here too!' Vandiyadevan said.

The child looked at the horse.

'Oho! You've brought the horse for me, have you? But they told me they would bring me a palanquin!'

The child's retorts triggered a series of contradicting thoughts in Vandiyadevan's mind. Who was this child? Why was he here all by himself? And what a wonder it was for such a little boy, barely out of infancy, to be so intrepid under such circumstances! And who had told him they would bring him a palanquin? Why was it not here yet? Who was the mother who had left him here? Where had she gone?

'My child, why has your Amma left you here by yourself?' Vandiyadevan asked.

'Amma did not leave me. I left her and came away,' the boy said.

'Why did you leave here?'

'A horse came running my way. I said I would catch the horse and come riding on it. Amma said I should not do that. I slipped away when she wasn't looking, to catch the horse by myself. Is this the horse I saw?'

'No, that's a different horse. But tell me, how did you come here?'

'I wasn't able to find the horse. I couldn't find my mother either. It was pouring. So, I took shelter in this ruin.'

'But aren't you afraid to stay in the dark by yourself?'

'Why would I be afraid? I live like this all the time!'

'You're not afraid of even tigers?'

'Only Amma is afraid. I'm not. I'm a fish. I will swallow tigers.'

'Ade! Fish swallow tigers?'

'I'm not an ordinary little fish! I am a makara meen, a crocodile fish. I am a whale! I will swallow tigers and lions and elephants, all!'

All sorts of thoughts were running through Vandiyadevan's head. Who had taught this child such things? A fish, a special fish, a crocodile fish or a whale, that could swallow tigers ...

'What's that noise?' the boy asked.

Vandiyadevan turned. He could see a group in the distance. Some of the party were holding torches aloft. A palanquin was being carried along too. They were running forward, as if in panic. A woman seemed to be among them.

'Here!'

'There!'

'This way!'

'That way!'

Everyone was shouting. Someone pointed towards the ruin. With that, they all began to run towards it.

'Oh, there they are, with the palanquin too. I don't want to ride the palanquin. Will you take me on your horse?' the child asked.

His face, appearance, mien, manner of speech had all captured Vandiyadevan's heart. He wanted to hold the child close to himself, and carry the boy in his arms. But something made him hesitate too.

'But I'm on an urgent mission myself,' Vandiyadevan said.

'Where are *you* going?'

'To Kanchi.'

'Kanchi? That's where my greatest enemy is!'

Vandiyadevan nearly jumped out of his skin. He sensed that it was dangerous to remain. But he didn't have the time to make a run for it either. The crowd that was running towards them had nearly reached then. And if he were to rush to his horse now, he would arouse their suspicions. Also, he was curious about the scenes that would play themselves out here. He settled for taking a few steps back so that he would be hidden in the shadows.

'Here I am!' the boy declared, stepping out of the ruin into the open, arms akimbo.

The first to reach him was the woman. She was panting from the run. But she dove forward nevertheless and scooped him up in her arms.

'Pandiya! What a thing to do!' she cried.

Next came Ravidasan. He came and stood by the boy and said, 'Chakravarti! What a fright you gave us!'

The boy laughed. 'And I will do it again!' he said. 'I asked for a horse. You've brought me a palanquin instead.'

Soman Saambavan, Idumbankaari and the Devaraalan, with all of whom the readers are already acquainted, followed. They surrounded the boy.

'Chakravarti! A single horse? Why, we'll bring you a thousand, ten thousand horses. But just for today, please get inside the palanquin,' Soman Saambavan said.

'No, I will not. I will ride that horse,' the boy said, pointing at Vandiyadevan's horse.

It was then that they noticed the horse and Vandiyadevan, who was standing by his ride.

Ravidasan's face was a sight. Shock, rage and fear fought for supremacy as his expression shifted constantly.

He took a couple of steps forward and said, 'Ada paavi! How did you get here?'

'Ada pisaase! How did you get here from Kodikkarai?' Vandiyadevan asked.

Ravidasan howled with laughter. 'Did you really think I was a pisaasu?' he asked.

'Some people are obliged to die before they turn into pisaasus. You've managed to do it while still alive,' Vandiyadevan said.

'Don't fight with him,' the boy said. 'I like him very much. He kept me company in the darkness. He said he would kill any tigers that came here. Let him come with us!'

Ravidasan went close to the boy and said, 'Chakravarti! We will certainly take him too. But, please, just for today, get into the palanquin!'

The boy made for the palanquin.

Ravidasan went up to Vandiyadevan and demanded, 'What will you do now?'

'That's for you to say, isn't it?'

'Come with us. You already knew too much. And now you know more. We can't leave you here. Come along.'

'And if I refuse?'

'You cannot. I know you're a great warrior. But there are twenty of us. You cannot possibly get away.'

'You mean I cannot get away alive, don't you?'

'You're young. You're yet to experience the world's joys and comforts. Why pointlessly lose your life now?'

'Who will lose his life pointlessly? Right, so you ask me to come with you, but where?'

'Good question. To the Pazhuvoor Ilaiya Rani.'

'Oho! It's as I thought, then. Where is the Ilaiya Rani?'

'I think she ought to have reached Tiruppurambiyam by now. Are you coming or not?'

'I have to go that way myself. I was just ruing the fact that there was no one around to point me in the right direction. Your arrival is timely. Come, let's go,' Vandiyadevan said.

By this time, the child had mounted the palanquin. Ravidasan's companions yelled out various cheers and cries as they carried him forward. Vandiyadevan joined them, accompanied by his thoughts. What had become of Vanathi? He had no clue. What had become of Madurantakan? He had no clue. What was to become of him tonight? He had no clue.

Clearly, he was set to uncover a far greater conspiracy than the one he had chanced upon at the Kadambur palace. Well, that was all very useful, but what would become of him afterwards? Would they let him get away alive? They would compel him to switch allegiances and join forced with them. If he refused, they would kill him. Perhaps, just once more, Nandini's compassion would ... it struck Vandiyadevan that the moment Ravidasan had mentioned the Pazhuvoor Ilaiya Rani, he had agreed to go along. He had been surprised by his own, instinctive reaction. Perhaps this was the 'maya' and the 'moham' the elders spoke of. He knew of the terrible conspiracies in which she was involved. And yet, when an opportunity to meet her presented itself, he was not able to resist. He felt helplessly eager to see her. Even before he had had a chance to weigh his options, his lips had uttered, 'Come, let's go', as if they'd had a mind of their own.

Then again, what options had he had? Ravidasan was right. He could not take on twenty men. There was a chance he might find a way to escape them. And in the meantime, he would get to know these conspirators and their plans better.

Kanchi? That's where my greatest enemy is!

The child's utterance, in his high-pitched, lisping voice, came to his mind every now and again. Who was the child? And why did these people address him as 'Chakravarti'? Who was the 'greatest enemy' to whom the boy had referred? Answers appeared in his mind too. The more he thought about it, the scarier it all seemed. Kadavule! What was all this building up to? How would everything end? And when?

Soon, very soon, said a voice in his head.

The strange procession with its palanquin went on and on, past fields and ditches and ponds and canals and valley and forest, without stopping for a moment. Finally, they crossed the gushing Manni river, and reached the border of Tiruppurambiyam. And then, they entered the forest before them.

13

'THE TIME IS NIGH!'

We've been here before, this pallipadai temple which had been built a century earlier and was now a ruin. This was the spot where Azhvarkadiyaan had hidden and eavesdropped on Ravidasan and his band of fellow conspirators. Now, we find ourselves here again, with Vandiyadevan and the rest.

They brought Vandiyadevan and his horse to a corner of the ruin.

'Appane! You stay right here until we call for you. Don't even dream of an escape. Nobody can enter or get out of this forest except for those who know it like we do. If you try, you'll die trying!' Ravidasan said.

'And even if I do find the way out, you'll cast one of your spells on me and kill me, won't you? You're a mantravadi, aren't you?' Vandiyadevan said, with a laugh.

'Laugh, laugh … laugh all you want,' Ravidasan said, and laughed too.

At that very moment, a jackal began to howl in the distance. Right after, an owl hooted. Vandiyadevan's hair stood on end. Not from the cold but from the sense that this forest was so forbidding that even the breeze was hesitant to venture inside. Why, even the rain hadn't dared pour here. As they had passed through the undergrowth, he had been surprised by how dry it was. There were barely a few drops of rain on the odd shrub.

It was stuffy in there. Vandiyadevan's waistcloth had dried by the time they reached the pallipadai. Only the cloth scroll he'd secured in his waistband was still wet. He spread it out to dry on a rock, and then sat on another rock and leaned against the wall. A lone man stood guarding him.

The rest of the men stood some distance away in a clearing. A man brought an old throne from the pallipadai and placed it there.

They sat the child whom they addressed as 'Chakravarti' on this throne. They then put out all the flares, but for two. The smoke from the doused flares spread in every direction.

'Why isn't the Rani here yet?' a man asked.

'She has to choose the right time, doesn't she? I have asked her to come during the second jaamam too. Until she does, someone sing songs in praise of the Vazhudi clan!' Soman Saambavan said.

Idumbankari produced an udukku drum, and began to tap it in time.

The Devaraalan began to sing.

Vandiyadevan saw and heard all this from where he sat. He knew that the 'Vazhudi clan' referred to the Pandiyas. The song sounded like some sort of lament. The beat of the udukku and the tune of the song made him rather sad. He was able to catch some of the lyrics and he gathered it was a song that recounted the war that had played out at that very spot a century earlier.

There had been a fierce three-day battle between Varaguna Pandiyan and Aparajita Pallavan. The Ganga king Prithvipati had arrived to aid the Pallava king, and had lost his life on the battlefield. The pallipadai that had been raised in his honour was the one that now served as the conspirators' den.

Prithvipati's martyrdom was also the death knell for the Pallavas. With their armies scattered, a Pandiya victory seemed certain. It was then that the Chozhas came to the aid of the Pallavas. At the vanguard was Vijayalaya Chozhan, the bearer of ninety-six scars. He was an old man who had lost the use of his legs, but was borne into the battlefield by four soldiers. In each hand, he wielded a mighty sword. As he let out a battle roar, he spun the swords into a blur. To those who watched him, it was as if he was spinning the discus of Vishnu. Everywhere he went, the Pandiya soldiers on either side of him fell as corpses to the ground.

The fleeing Pallava armies returned to the battlefield inspired by the Chozha emperor.

'Jana jana jana janaar!' Ten thousand swords shone in the gloaming of the evening sun!

'Dana dana dana danaar!' Ten thousand spears sparkled silver as they flew through the air!

The swords and spears clashed. A hundred thousand heads fell to the ground, and a hundred thousand headless bodies fell, too.

'Ee ee ee ee,' the horses neighed as they fell dead.

'Plee plee plee plee,' elephants trumpeted as they fell dead.

It was a flood, not of water but blood, a red river carrying dead people and animals. Twenty thousand carrion birds flew overhead, turning the blue sky black. Thirty thousand jackals came howling to the battlefield.

'Aiyo! O! O!' fifty thousand voices rose in a wail.

'Don't let them go! Catch them! Chase them! Slay them! Slice them!' a hundred thousand men roared.

'Ad-dum! Ad-dum! Ad-dum!' ten thousand victory drums boomed.

'Ploo! Ploo! Ploo!' twenty thousand conches blew.

'Ha! Ha! Ha!' sixty thousand ghosts laughed.

Vandiyadevan woke with a start. He blinked and looked about himself. He realised he had dozed off, leaning against the wall of the pallipadai. In his half-sleep, he replayed the terrifying dream he'd had. Was it a dream? No! It must be images triggered by the song the Devaraalan was singing.

At that moment, the man was recounting the scene of the Pallava and Ganga armies fleeing before the might of the Pandiyas. His audience was laughing with glee, and it was the sound of this awful laughter that had morphed into the ghosts' mirth in Vandiyadevan's dream and woken him. All of a sudden, Idumbankaari stopped playing the drum. The Devaraalan's song faded into silence.

A flare was moving towards them from some distance away. In its light, they could see a palanquin approaching. The bearers set it down. The curtains of the palanquin parted. A woman stepped outside. Yes, she was indeed the Pazhuvoor Rani, Nandini.

Vandiyadevan had only ever seen her in silk and ornaments, glowing like the goddess Mohini. Now, she appeared with her long hair fallen loose, the picture of the avenging goddess Ugra Durga. Vandiyadevan's heart stopped. His entire body began to tremble.

As Nandini walked towards the gathering, her eyes were focused on the child sitting on the throne. The child, too, looked at her. Everyone else stared at them both.

The woman who had come running in search of the child in the ruin——the woman whom he had addressed as 'Amma'——stood behind the throne.

As Nandini neared the boy, she held out both arms.

The boy looked back and forth between her and the woman standing behind him.

'You are my mother, aren't you? Not her?' the boy asked.

'Yes, kanmani![1]' the Pazhuvoor Rani said.

'Then why does she call herself my mother?'

'She is your foster mother, the mother who raised you.'

'Why didn't you raise me? Why didn't you keep me with you? Why is she hiding me in some mountain cave?'

'Kanmani! This is to fulfil your father's desires. To take revenge against his murderers!'

'Yes, I know that,' the boy said, and jumped off the throne.

Nandini gathered him in her waiting arms and kissed the top of his head. The boy hugged her tight, as if he wanted to make sure she never left him again.

But this did not last. Nandini forcibly freed herself from the little arms that held her, and seated the boy back on the throne.

She walked to the palanquin and reached inside. She pulled out the sword we have seen before, once in the blacksmith's hands and once in her own. She gestured to the palanquin bearers, who then carried the palanquin some distance away and sat down by it, hidden from view.

Nandini approached the throne again, and placed the sword so it rested on the throne's arms.

The boy stared at it in fascination and then said, 'May I hold it?'

'Have some patience, my kanmani!' Nandini said. Then, she looked at Ravidasan and the rest, squinting her eyes as she put a name to each face. 'There is no one here other than those who have sworn the oath, is there?'

'No, devi!' Ravidasan said.

Nandini turned to him.

'Senapati ...' she began, only to be interrupted by his laughter.

'The title amuses you today. Who knows what will happen this day, next month?'

'Devi! How long we have been waiting for that day, wondering when it will be?'

'Aiyo, we're a handful of warriors. Our Chakravarti is a child. The Chozha empire is enormous, with a strong army. If we had hurried our mission, we would have been ruined. It is our patience that had brought us to this position—our mission will be accomplished shortly, the time is nigh! Ravidasare! Is there anything you wish to say? Is there anything anyone else wishes to say?'

Ravidasan glanced at the faces of his men, all of whom seemed content in their silence.

'Devi, there is nothing we have to say. But you have to tell us what you mean by "the time is nigh". Where, how and through whom will our mission be accomplished? Do grace us with this information too!'

'Indeed. I have come here expressly to tell you this. That is why I asked all of you to gather here and wait. And I asked that our Chakravarti be brought here too.'

Everyone, including the child on the throne, was looking at Nandini's face.

'Some among you were in a hurry,' she said. 'Some of you suspected that I might have forgotten the oath we took. That suspicion is baseless. I have more reason than any of you to remember that oath. I have not forgotten it. I have spent every day and every night of the last three years thinking of nothing else. Nothing else but how to create the opportune circumstance and moment, how to trap whom and for what, in order to accomplish our mission, in order to fulfil our promise, in order to keep our oath. The circumstances are finally right. The moment is here. The suzerain kings and great warriors of Chozha Naadu have split into two factions. Pazhuvettaraiyar, Sambuvarayar and some others have decided Madurantakan must be crowned the next king. Kodumbalur Boothi Vikrama Kesari and Tirukkovalur Malayaman are opposed to this. I hear that Boothi Vikrama Kesari is marching on Thanjai with the army of the Southern Front, while Malayaman is gathering his men too. Civil war could break out at any moment.'

'Devi! We hear that you're going to great pains to avert this civil war. We hear that there will be peace talks in Kadambur Sambuvarayar's palace.'

'Yes, it is true that I have made these arrangements. But do you not see why?'

'No, we don't. Rani! A woman's heart cannot be read even by Sarveshwara, according to the elders. How can we ordinary mortals read yours?'

'True, you cannot. Let me explain. If civil war were to break out before our mission is accomplished, the outcome is not predictable. Sundara Chozhan is still alive. That cunning Anbil Brahmarayan is around too. These two men will intervene and calm down both factions. Or, one faction will emerge victorious, in which case we will not be able to fulfil our promise. That is why I have organised these peace talks. We must see our task through before the civil war actually breaks out. Once we achieve our goal, there will be no end to this civil war. Not until both sides are decimated. Do you now see why I have initiated these peace talks?'

The faces of the men betrayed their surprise and excitement. They couldn't help murmuring among themselves how incredible the Pazhuvoor Rani's foresight was. Even Ravidasan couldn't help admiring her plan.

'Devi! We are stunned by your foresight. We have now understood why you've called for peace talks. But then, you said the time is nigh, that our mission will soon be accomplished. Who will put it into action? How? When?' he asked.

'That will happen alongside the peace talks. An invitation has been sent under this pretext to our main foe, to attend these talks at the Kadambur palace. He will be there without a doubt. And that is where we will fulfil our oath. O Veerapandiya Chakravarti's Abaththudavigal! The time is nigh for you to avenge the injustice! Today is Sanikizhamai[2], isn't it? By next Sanikizhamai, our oath will be realised!'

All twenty people gathered there let out a war cry. Some jumped for joy. Idumbankaari drummed twice on the udukku. This woke the sleeping owls and sent them scurrying towards the higher branches. Bats flapped their wings and flew past. Vandiyadevan's horse shook himself nervously.

Vandiyadevan, too, stood up.

All he could tell from the distance was that Nandini had said something that had excited the people she was addressing. He hadn't heard her words.

Ravidasan gestured for everyone to calm down.

'Devi! Your last words have given us immense joy! We cannot believe that we have but a week to go to kill our foe and avenge our emperor! But who will have the honour?'

'It is natural that all of us should compete for this honour. And it is to ensure that this decision is made without anyone feeling upset that I have asked for our Chakravarti, the son of Veerapandiyar, to be present. Veerapandiyar's sword, too, is here. Whomever this little child hands his father's sword to will be the one who must avenge Veerapandiyar. And everyone else must stand at the ready. If the person chosen by our Chakravarti is not able to accomplish the task, everyone else must step in. I will be inside the Kadambur palace.

Idumbankaari will be among the palace guards. We will help the chosen one enter the palace. Do I have everyone's consent for these arrangements?'

The men looked at the faces around them. It appeared everyone was happy with the arrangements.

Ravidasan stepped forward, and said, 'Your arrangements are acceptable to us all. But there's another important issue. Whoever is chosen as our instrument of revenge will have supreme command here. Everyone must follow the chosen one's orders. Until our Chakravarti comes of age, whoever takes revenge will be the regent, and his word will be law.'

Nandini's face broke into a smile.

'And this includes me, yes?' she asked.

'Yes, devi. No exceptions can be made,' Ravidasan said.

'Excellent. Do I have everyone's consent for Ravidasan's proposal?' Nandini asked everyone else.

The men looked around again. They appeared hesitant to reply. One got the sense that some among them were not happy with the proposal.

Soman Saambavan said, 'How is that fair? How can our devi, who has done everything to aid us, be subject to the common man's word?'

'Please don't worry on my account. The only reason I am alive is to avenge the terrible murder of Veerapandiya Chakravarti. Whoever takes revenge will have my gratitude and servitude forever and ever,' Nandini said.

Then, she turned to the child who had been listening to all this, with or without comprehension, and said, 'Kanmani! This sword was your father's. Lift it with your little hands and give it to whomever you like most in this gathering.'

Ravidasan took a further step forward and said, 'Chakravarti, look at each one of us carefully! Whoever strikes you as the bravest and most courageous among us, hand the sword of the Pandiya clan to him!'

The infant emperor looked at every face around him, from his perch on the throne.

Everyone stared back at him, barely able to contain the excitement and anticipation of the moment.

Every pair of eyes pleaded: 'Pick me! Pick me!'

Ravidasan alone stared with an authoritative expression. His eyes and face did not plead, so much as command: 'Hand it to me!'

The child took his time. He gave each man the once-over a few times before placing his hands under the sword. It took him some effort to lift it.

The excitement of the group reached its peak.

The child swung round to face Nandini.

'Amma! You're the one I like most in this gathering. It is you who must rule on my behalf until I grow up!' he said, and handed over the sword to her.

14

A FIGURE IN THE DARK

Nandini stared at the sword being held out to her by the child who had been addressed as 'Chakravarti'. She then reached out to take it in her own hands, and pressed it to her chest. Then, she took the child in her arms and enveloped him in an embrace too. Tears were cascading down her cheeks.

The rest of the assembly looked on, too stunned to react for some time.

Ravidasan was the first to snap out of the spell.

'Devi! Our Chakravarti did not quite understand our request. He has given you the sword because of this incomprehension. We should explain again and ...'

Nandini interrupted him, and said in a grief-stricken voice, 'No, aiya, no! Chakravarti has given me the sword *because* he understood all that was said. It is your incomprehension that makes you worry. My tears are owed to the joy that I am the one who has been chosen for the honour of avenging the murder of Veerapandiya Chakravarti.'

'Devi! Give it some thought. There are so many of us Abaththudavigal, trained for ...' Soman Saambavan began, only to be interrupted by Nandini.

'There is no need for me to give this any thought. This is my responsibility. However, it is not as if you don't have your roles to play. I would like half of you to escort the Chakravarti to the Panchapandava hill. The rest of you will accompany me to Kadambur. Those who must be inside the palace will enter, and the rest of you must remain ready outside, with horses that can run fast. Once our mission is accomplished, it is imperative that we all get out of there alive,' Nandini said.

Ravidasan took another step forward and said, 'Ammani, I forgot to mention something. Please allow me to tell you.'

'Tell me, aiya, but make it fast. Pazhuvettaraiyar has gone to the Kalamukha Sangam on the banks of the Kollidam. I must be at the palace before he returns,' Nandini said.

'You said our sworn enemy Aditya Karikalan will be at the Kadambur palace, didn't you? That is not certain.'

'Why do you say that?'

'I have reason to believe so. A scroll is on its way to Aditya Karikalan, instructing him not to go to the Kadambur palace under any circumstances.

Pazhaiyarai Ilaiya Piraatti and Prime Minister Aniruddha Brahmarayar have sent him this message.'

'And you think I'm not aware of this?'

'You expect him to be at Kadambur in spite of it?'

'Yes, most certainly. That she-snake of Pazhaiyarai does not know Aditya Karikalan's nature. Neither does Anbil Brahmarakshasa. Neither do you, for all your knowledge of maya-mantra, your spells and incantations and powers of divination. If someone were to forbid him from doing something, Aditya Karikalar will definitely go and do it. I know this, I know this for sure. He is not a puppet like Arulmozhi Varman. And he is not a coward like Madurantakan. The fact that his sister and the prime minister have asked him not to go to Kadambur itself will spur him on to that very place.'

'Devi, you should not depend on that either. The scroll they have sent will not reach Kanchi,' Ravidasan said.

'What are you saying, aiya? Please explain,' Nandini said, her voice carrying a note of panic.

'Devi! Do you know who is carrying this scroll to Aditya Karikalan?' Ravidasan asked.

'I don't know for sure, but I can guess.'

'Well, you needn't. We have captured him. He was hiding in the same ruin where the Chakravarti had taken shelter from the rain. He knows all our secrets. We will be sabotaging ourselves if we let him leave alive. Idumbankaari! Bring that spy here!' Ravidasan said.

Idumbankaari went to the pallipadai temple, accompanied by two others.

Nandini squinted into the dark, trying to see what was happening there.

Her face, which had gone pale a few moments ago, was now back to glowing. A smile played on her lips.

The three men approached Vandiyadevan, who was leaning against a wall, half-asleep. They pounced on him. For a moment, the Vaanar scion wondered whether he should wrestle with them. Then, he decided against it. He was curious about what they intended to do. They bound his arms with a thick rope, and then wound it around his body. They pushed him forward, and brought him before Nandini.

Vandiyadevan smiled at the sight of the Pazhuvoor Ilaiya Rani, whose countenance withheld all emotion and appeared entirely calm.

'Aiya … yet again …' she began.

'Yes, devi, yet again, I've landed up before you! But it was not of my own accord,' he said, indicating the assembly around them.

The child standing by Nandini said, 'Amma! He's the one who saved me from the pisaasus in the dark. He made sure the pisaasu didn't eat me up. Why is he bound?'

Vandiyadevan turned to the child and said, 'Little boy, hush now! You must not interrupt when your elders are talking. Or, the tiger will eat you up!'

'I will eat the tiger up!' the boy said.

'Can a fish eat a tiger?' Vandiyadevan asked.

The men around him let out rasping noises from their throat. For a moment, the sound gave Vandiyadevan goosebumps.

'Devi, do you see?' Ravidasan said. 'We cannot let him get away alive. We allowed him to leave twice before, on your request. But we cannot abide by such a request this time round!'

'Mantravadi! Why do you lie? *You* allowed me to leave? It was *I* who escaped your clutches, wasn't it? Devi! Take a good look at the mantravadi and tell me … is he really Ravidasan? Or the ghost of Ravidasan?' Vandiyadevan asked.

Ravidasan roared with laughter. 'Yes, yes, I'm a ghost, a pisaasu,' he said. 'I'm going to drink your blood tonight!'

The men around him made the same throaty, rasping noise again.

The child said, 'Amma! He has a horse that I like very much. Ask him to give it to me!'

'Child, come with me! I'll take you on the horse,' Vandiyadevan said.

Ravidasan glared at Vandiyadevan and said, 'Ade! Shut up!' He then turned to Nandini and said, 'Devi! Give the order soon!'

Nandini asked calmly, 'How did he come here? And when?'

'This spy tried to kidnap the Chakravarti from the mandapam where he had taken shelter from the rain.

Thankfully, we arrived in time to stop him. If we had been a moment late, a terrible fate would have befallen our ...'

'Aiya! Are they telling the truth?' Nandini asked.

'It is you who should know whether your men are telling the truth, devi! How would *I* know?' Vandiyadevan said.

The smile that had lit up Nandini's face disappeared as suddenly as it had appeared. She turned to Ravidasan and said, 'Aiya, please move some distance away. I wish to speak to him in private.'

'Devi, it is late, and we are courting danger. Is this really the time ...'

Nandini interrupted him and said in an authoritative voice, 'Remind yourself of the condition to which we all agreed sometime ago. Now, move away without another word. And take the Chakravarti with you!' She then bent down and whispered into the child's ear, 'Kumara![1] Go with them. I'll speak to him and get you your horse.'

Ravidasan and the others hurried away without another word, taking the boy with them.

Nandini gave Vandiyadevan a once-over in the dim light of the small torch and said, 'Aiya! You and I appear to have some sort of bond.'

'Ammani! And it is a very capricious one! And a strong one too. Look how tightly that bond has bound me,' Vandiyadevan said.

'Leave your facetious talk aside for now. Did you intend to come here? Or was it a coincidence?'

'I didn't intend to come here. It was not a coincidence either, nor even a choice. It was your men who brought me here by force. Or I'd have been at the banks of the Kollidam by now.'

'I see you've been greatly troubled by this forced meeting with me. And I see how keen you are to leave too,' Nandini said.

'I'm not troubled by having met you. And I feel truly sorry to have to part from you. Just say the word. You're caught between that ancient Pazhuvettaraiyar on the one hand and this awful mantravadi on the other. Say the word, and I'll free you from them both and take you away!'

'Take me where?'

'I'll take you to your mother, who wanders the forests of Lanka like an orphan!'

Nandini let out a heavy sigh. 'Do you wish that I should wander like an orphan too? A time might very well come when I'll do that. And when it does, I will certainly seek your help to unite me with my mother. But my mission must be accomplished before such a time comes. Will you help me accomplish it?' she asked.

'Ammani, unless I know what your mission is, how can I tell you whether I will help?' Vandiyadevan asked.

'People who truly care for one will not insist on conditional help. They will promise help even without knowing what one's mission is.'

'Ammani, people who truly care for one will try to warn one in time and save one from danger. These scoundrels have hatched some conspiracy and got you mired in it. They simply want to use you to achieve their ends.'

'You're wrong. I am the one trying to use them to achieve my ends. Please understand that.'

'They've brought some little child from the forest and are trying to fool you.'

'Do you know what the child is for?'

'To be seated on the Pandiya throne so he can be crowned king,' Vandiyadevan said.

'Again, you're wrong. Not to be seated on the Pandiya throne alone. But on the throne of the empire that stretches from the Tungabhadra to Lanka—the Chozha throne.'

'Ammamma! And with whose help do you intend to accomplish such a forbidding mission? With the help of this pack of jackals? The Chozha army has ten divisions, each comprising 2,00,000 trained warriors who can take on multiple enemies. And you intend to beat them with the help of these ten–twenty jackals who hide during the day and emerge at night?'

'I'm not counting on them alone. Here, I have this sword in my hand. With the help of this sword, I will fulfil the task to which I have set my mind.'

'Ammani! You're never going to use that sword. The strength that one needs to wield it can be found neither in your arms, nor in your heart.'

'Why do you say that?'

'It's how I feel.'

'I can prove that you are wrong, right here, right now.'

'In that case, I will count myself blessed. One must have done something good to have earned the honour of death at your lovely hands,' Vandiyadevan said. With that, he bent his neck low as if ready for a beheading, his face turned to the ground.

'Is having your head lopped off by my lovely hands all that you desire? You don't wish to adorn your head with a crown?' Nandini asked.

'How many people do you intend to crown king?'

'That's up to me. Whoever I feel truly deserves the crown in the end will wear it.'

'Then what about that little boy?'

'It's all up to me, isn't it? Whether I crown him king or not is my wish, isn't it?'

'Devi, please crown whoever you wish to. I have no desire for a crown.'

'Why?'

'Many people have praised my curly hair. A crown would ruin this much-admired hairstyle. I don't wish for that to happen.'

'You'll never stop your banter, no matter how serious an issue we're discussing. Well, then! So, what did Ilaiya Piraatti do when she heard that Ponniyin Selvan had drowned at sea? Was she very sad?' Nandini asked, suddenly changing the subject.

Vandiyadevan was startled. He recovered quickly, and said, 'How can one not be sad? Are all women heartless?'

'I believe that Kodumbalur girl tried to drown herself to death in the lake. Is that true? Who saved her life?'

Vandiyadevan suddenly remembered that he had no idea what had become of Vanathi after her entourage had been accosted. He was so preoccupied with his thoughts that he forgot that Nandini had asked him something.

Nandini said, her voice suddenly hard, 'All right, I knew you wouldn't answer that. Are you going to prevent Aditya Karikalar from coming to the Kadambur palace?'

'I'm going to try,' Vandiyadevan said.

'I say you can't.'

'I don't say I can either, devi. All I said is that I'm going to try. Once the prince has made up his mind about something, it's not easy to change it.'

'You understand Aditya Karikalar's nature well.'

'You know him better than I do.'

'Well … however much I ask, you refuse to join forces with me. You will remain in my enemy's camp. That's how it is, isn't it?'

'Ammani! Who is your enemy?'

'Who is my enemy? The Pazhaiyarai princess, who else!'

'That is your imagination, devi. I have to tell you a truth, an important truth …'

'Enough, aiya, enough. Don't I know enough about your idea of the truth? If you claim something is the truth, it will be distilled lies of the most exquisite quality. You can keep your truth to yourself. I don't want it!' Nandini said, and clapped her hands.

Ravidasan and the rest appeared right away and began to close in on Vandiyadevan, who realised he hadn't made full use of the opportunity he had been given. This rakshashi was going to order them to kill him right away. What a fate! Instead of a glorious death on the battlefield, he was going to die at the hands of these scoundrels in the middle of nowhere. The group had now surrounded him, making the same rasping noise. He was reminded of a pack of wolves slurping as they surrounded their prey.

'Rani! I knew he wouldn't fall in line, whatever you said. Leave right away. We'll offer him as a sacrifice in this holy place,' Ravidasan said.

'Mantravadi! Watch your words. That is not my will. None of you should harm this gentleman in any manner. If anyone so much as lays a hand on him, I will slice that man to bits with this sword!' Nandini roared.

Ravidasan and the rest stepped back, stunned.

'I have much work for him. Do you understand? I'm leaving now. You leave too. Let him go where he pleases. No one will stop him!' Nandini said.

'Devi! I have a request. We'll do as you wish. But he has a horse. Is it wise to let him get a head start on us? Think about it ...'

'All right, tie him to that temple pillar. It will take him a while to free himself. By then, you'll be out of this forest.'

Vandiyadevan was bound to the pillar at the temple. His horse was tied to a tree, some distance away. Nandini left on her palanquin. Ravidasan and his men hurried away with the little boy. The flame they carried grew smaller as they walked further away, and eventually disappeared, leaving Vandiyadevan in the dark.

He wondered whether everything he had seen and heard had been a dream after all. Enormous bats flapped their wings as they flew through the mandapam. Owls hooted and murmured. Jackals howled through the night. Vandiyadevan had a sense that they were closing in on him as they howled. Silhouettes flitted through the dark, shapeless beings with formless plans.

The nightmare he'd had at the Kadambur palace came to mind, as if a thousand jackals were about to tear him to pieces and drink his blood. The thought sent shivers down Vandiyadevan's spine, and he hurried to free himself from the ropes. That was not an easy task. If it had been light, he could have seen where the knots were. In the darkness, he had to feel his way around them. Even if the dark clouds had parted and the stars were out in the night sky, the canopy of trees above him made it impossible for the starlight to penetrate the forest.

Aha! What was that sound? Well, the jungle was full of beasts. Why should a sound surprise him? No, no, this was no beast. It sounded like human feet. His horse neighed, and then began to shift its weight from one hoof to another, as if agitated. Was it some dangerous animal, a tiger perhaps? Vandiyadevan struggled against the ropes. It was of no use.

A figure appeared. A dark shadow in the dark night. Was it a human figure? Or ... what else could it be? It was approaching him.

Vandiyadevan fortified himself to face whatever was coming. And gathered all his strength and focused it on his legs. When the figure was close enough, he aimed a sharp kick at it. It went flying back with a cry. Then, there was a 'danaar' sound. It must have hit the wall of the shrine.

The figure remained some distance away. It appeared to be leaning against the temple wall. Vandiyadevan could not see too well in the dark, but he had the sense that the creature was staring at him.

He tried even harder to undo the ropes. Those mantravadi pisaasus had done a thorough job with the knots. Well, he would teach Ravidasan a lesson the next time they met.

The figure moved now. It seemed to be going into the pallipadai temple. Soon after, there was a repeated 'dan-dan' sound, as if pebbles were rolling against each other.

A light appeared outside the temple. Yes, the figure was holding a small torch. It was approaching Vandiyadevan now. It was a Kalamukha Veerashaivite. A long beard, matted locks, a necklace of skulls ... yes, a Kalamukha indeed. The figure came close to Vandiyadevan, held up the torch and studied his face in its light.

15

A DISGUISE EXPOSED

The terrifying aspect of the Kalamukha had Vandiyadevan frozen for a moment. But then, his natural daring drove away his fear, and he began to think. Had he not seen this man before? He had ... but where? Yes, he was one of the two men who had walked past Vandiyadevan when he had been pretending to sleep by the banks of the Arichandra river. But was it just the once that he had seen this face before? There was something about the Kalamukha's eyes ... those sharp eyes with their piercing stare, surely Vandiyadevan had seen them elsewhere too?

The Shaivite took a long look at him and then laughed. Surely, he had heard this laugh before too?

'Ada chhe! It's you, after all, is it? Was it for you that I came all this way taking so much trouble in the middle of the night?' the Kalamukha said. It appeared to Vandiyadevan that the man had altered his voice slightly.

'Then, whom else did you come for?' Vandiyadevan asked.

'I came in search of the prince.'

'Which prince?'

'How does it matter to you? Why do you ask?'

'I'm a prince too, that's why.'

'Some prince! Look at the face of this "prince"!'

'Why, what's wrong with my face, aiya? Will my face benefit from a moustache and matted locks and beard and skull necklace, do you think?'

'Maybe you should try that look, and then you'll know.'

'How long will it take to grow all that hair?'

'Oh, why's that even a factor? A day, if you wish. Even a naazhigai will do.'

'I thought as much.'

'What did you think?'

'Nothing. Undo these ropes first. I'll join your group.'

'No, no, thank you very much. There's already a spy like you in our group. That's why our mahasangam ended as it did.'

'How did it end?'

'We were expecting the prince at the mahasangam. We thought he was going to announce that once he had ascended to the throne, he would institute our mahaguru as the Rajguru. But the prince didn't show up.'

'Free me from these ropes. I'll tell you why the prince did not come.'

'Which prince?'

'Which prince could it possibly be? Kandaradityar's son Madurantakar, who else?'

'It's as I thought.'

'What did you think?'

'I was referring to my having deduced that you were a spy.'

'How did you deduce that?'

'As I was coming here in search of the prince, I saw some people leaving the forest. I know who they are. They must have figured out that you're a spy and tied you up. But I don't see why they left you alive.'

'I'll tell you. Now, undo these ropes!'

'You don't have to tell me anything. And I won't undo these ropes either. If you do as I say ...'

'If I do *what* as you say?'

'If you agree not to poke your nose into matters that don't concern you, and then do a hundred and eight thoppukaranams[1] ...'

'Is that how it is, then?'

All through the repartee, Vandiyadevan's hands had been working to undo the ropes that bound him. The last knot had come off just as the Kalamukha was saying, '... do a hundred and eight thoppukaranams.'

Vandiyadevan pounced on the Kalamukha and took him down. The torch fell to the ground, but did not go out completely.

He then sat on the chest of the Kalamukha, who was flat on his back against the ground, and tugged at his beard. It came off in his hands. The Kalamukha pushed Vandiyadevan off and sat up.

Vandiyadevan reached for the torch and held it up to the Kalamukha's face. Now that it had been ridden of its beard and locks, it had transformed into the familiar face of the Veera Vaishnavite Azhvarkadiyaan.

The two of them looked at each other and laughed.

'Vaishnavare! You told me not to poke my nose into matters that were not my concern? And look at what you're doing!' Vandiyadevan asked.

'But I don't get into scrapes like you do. If I hadn't arrived here when I did ...'

'Do you believe it was you who undid the ropes?'

'You might have undone your ropes. But you'll be undone without me. You can't find your way out of this forest without my help. You'll fall prey to the jackals.'

'Well, speaking of jackals ... that mantravadi and his band ... it's something that I got away from *that* band of jackals, isn't it?'

'I know them well enough. Was it only the mantravadi and his crew that came? Or someone else along with them?'

'A little fish came. A magic fish that believes it can swallow tigers whole.'

'Aha! Tell me, tell me. Who all were here? And what exactly happened?'

'Why did you don this disguise? Where did you head off in the evening? And what happened where you went? If you tell me all that I'll tell you what happened here.'

'I don't have much to say. The Kalamukha mahasangam was held tonight at the banks of the Kollidam. I donned this disguise to find out what was happening there. I figured I would meet you at the boat bay after. The mahasangam gathered. Periya Pazhuvettaraiyar was there. The mahaguru of the Kalamukhas was there too. But the man whose arrival they were all anticipating did not show up.'

'Prince Madurantakar?'

'Yes. But how did you know?'

'If Madurantakar were to ascend to the Thanjai throne, some governance we'll have!'

'What makes you say that?'

'He isn't able to tame and control a lone horse. How will he deal with suzerain kings like the Pazhuvettaraiyar brothers and frightening Kalamukha Shaivites and quarrelsome Veera Vaishnavites?'

Azhvarkadiyaan laughed and said, 'Did you see Madurantakar on your way here? Do you know what became of him?'

Vandiyadevan told him about how he had seen Madurantakar, how the prince's horse had reared up at the sight of a torch, how he had gone in search of Madurantakan and how he had eventually seen the horse without its rider. Vandiyadevan finished his narrative with, 'Aiyo, paavam! Who knows where the horse has thrown him? His very life could be in danger.

That's why he didn't turn up at your mahasangam. Should we go in search of him again?'

'Who cares about him? How is it of any concern to us? Come, we have a mission to complete. Start moving! We must reach the boat bay of the Kollidam river before dawn!' Azhvarkadiyaan said.

'But what if Madurantakar is lying dead in some canal or field? Would you say that is no concern of ours?'

'Nothing of that sort will happen. Aniruddhar would have taken precautions.

'The prime minister Aniruddhar? What does he have to do with this? How would he even know what happened?'

'Aha! What a question! Nothing happens anywhere in the empire without Anbil Aniruddhar knowing about it.'

'Oho! So, he knows about the conspiracy plotted at the Kadambur palace?'

'You'd do well to keep something in mind. Do you remember, during the temple festival at Veeranarayanapuram, the two of us saw the palanquin of the Pazhuvoor Rani pass by?'

'Yes, and when the curtain parted, I saw how flustered you got. And then you asked me if I would hand over a scroll to the Pazhuvoor Rani!'

'And you said, "Chhi chhi! What a thing to ask!" You figured I was writing her a love letter. All I wanted to do was write, "Don't be swayed by the talk of conspirators. If you trust them, you will court destruction", and hand it over to Madurantakar, as per the prime minister's instructions.'

'You knew the person inside the palanquin was Madurantakar?'

'At first, I suspected it might be. My suspicions were confirmed when the curtain parted. You're something, though ... I tried so hard to draw you out, and yet you refused to tell me that the occupant of the palanquin was Madurantakan and not the Pazhuvoor Rani!'

'You're not so bad yourself, are you? You wouldn't even tell me where you were going last evening!'

'If I had, you'd have insisted on interfering in that mission too. Look at what a mess you've made for yourself already! At least make sure, in the future, you ...'

'Does the prime minister know about the Kalamukha mahasangam and Madurantakar's plans of being present?'

'Why would he have sent me if he hadn't known about it? At the same time, he would have made arrangements to ensure Madurantakar couldn't be there. You said a man appeared with a torch, didn't you? He must have been sent by Aniruddhar. It would have been his intention to scare the horse. Someone would have rescued the prince after he was thrown off. He must be on his way to Thanjai in a chariot or palanquin by now. Come, let's be on our way too.'

'Vaishnavare! I can't come with you.'

'What is this? What will become of your mission? I hear that Aditya Karikalar has left Kanchi. We must fly like the wind to ...'

'You can pass on the scroll to Aditya Karikalar yourself, can't you? He won't wear the disguise of a woman as Madurantakar did. Neither will he slink by at night.'

'And what do *you* intend to do?'

'To be honest, it was not in pursuit of Madurantakar that I went this evening. I was going in search of someone else, when I happened to see Madurantakar.'

'If you'll allow me a prediction ... I'd say it was a woman you were pursuing.'

'You've got a filthy mind, Vaishnavare! One day, I'm going to split that head open and clean it up!'

'You can't do that. I've already pledged my head to a Kalamukha. Well, that's as it may be. Who was it you pursued from Kudandai? Who was that lady?'

'The Kodumbalur princess had come to the house of the astrologer in Kudandai. She left alone on the palanquin. To be honest, I did not go in search of that crazy woman. Her palanquin was going ahead of me for a while. All of a sudden, some people attacked the palanquin. They tied her maid to a tree, and left with Vanathi alone. Vaishnavare! I can't possibly come with you without knowing what became of that girl.'

'And why are you so worried about that girl?'

'What a thing to say! Isn't she the daughter of the great martyr of the Eezham battlefield, Kodumbalur

Siriya Velaar? And the dearest friend of Pazhaiyarai Ilaiya Piraatti? And aren't there plans afoot to get her married to Ponniyin Selvar?'

'Appane! But Ponniyin Selvar has drowned to death, hasn't he? Why are you concerned with this wedding now?'

'There is no confirmation of his death. It is all conjecture, isn't it?'

'So, you think he's alive?'

'Vaishnavare! If you intend to draw me out and get me to reveal some secret, you can forget about it.'

'All right, all right. I know you're a vault. But you don't have to worry on account of Vanathi Devi. You know she means the world to Ilaiya Piraatti, don't you?'

'That's why I'm worried. Ilaiya Piraatti might not know Vanathi Devi is in danger, no?'

'If she doesn't know yet, she'll know soon.'

'What's the point of knowing too late? What if the Kalamukhas offer that girl as a sacrifice tonight?'

'Are you saying it was the Kalamukhas who kidnapped Vanathi?'

'That's what I think. Her maid said the same thing.'

'If that's true, you need not worry at all. The Kodumbalur family have deep ties with the Kalamukhas. Once they know Vanathi is a Kodumbalur princess, the Kalamukhas will treat her with all the deference due to royalty.'

'Oho! I had no idea!'

'That is why the Kalamukhas are now against Madurantaka Devar.'

'So what if those skull-bearers are against him?'

'Another thing you have no idea about. Most of the grand families of this empire are aligned with the Kalamukhas. So are many of those in the army. That is why Pazhuvettaraiyar has made these arrangements. All in the hope that the Kalamukhas will support Madurantakar. That plan came to nothing thanks to a horse. So, are you coming with me, or shall I go on my way?'

Vandiyadevan got up with a heavy sigh and took his horse's reins. They found their way through the dense forest and emerged on the other side.

'Look!' Azhvarkadiyaan said, pointing at the sky.

The tail of the Dhoomaketu seemed longer than ever. It extended for an entire half of the night sky. A cold wind hit them at that moment, and Vandiyadevan shivered involuntarily.

Far away, a lone dog raised a sorrowful howl.

16

WHAT BECAME OF VANATHI

As the sun sank into the horizon and the dark hood of night covered the earth, Vanathi's palanquin was being carried on the road that connected Kudandai and Tiruvarur. Her mind was in turmoil. She was aching to go to the Nagapattinam Choodamani Vihara and nurse the prince back to health. But how would she achieve this? Would the Buddhist monks allow her inside the vihara? Would she be able to meet the prince? And even if she did, would she be permitted to sit by his bedside? Even as these doubts gnawed at her, the idea of having to make this journey without an escort or bodyguard ate away at her courage. She tried to steel herself. Nothing in the world could be achieved easily, could it now? People put tremendous effort into achieving their ends, didn't they? If a boatwoman could ply her craft all alone in the sea, how courageous must she be? She had navigated a storm and rain and waves the size of mountains to rescue the prince, hadn't she? If Vanathi's rival was such a braveheart, how could the princess afford to be intimidated by a short journey by road?

So what if they did not allow her into the vihara? She would stay somewhere nearby, where she could have news of the prince. And so what if she could not meet the prince? She would be able to get a look at that boatwoman, at the very least. Yes, that was the right thing to do. She would get to know the boatwoman, and perhaps she would be able to find an opportunity to meet the prince through *her*. Vanathi's love for the prince must come of some use, surely? Surely, she would be able to nurse him back to health? Once he was all right, she would be happy to die. Or join the Buddhist order.

She parted the curtains and leaned out, to ask the palanquin bearers when they would reach Nagapattinam. She thought she saw some figures hiding among the trees that grew by the road. She squinted at them, and realised they were Veerashaiva Kalamukhas. But that did not trouble Vanathi. Growing up in the Kodumbalur palace, she had often seen Kalamukhas visit the court. They would seek out her uncle, and leave with whatever they had asked for. Their mahaguru himself had once visited Kodumbalur. He was given a grand welcome and honoured with various pujas. Her uncle Boothi Vikrama Kesari had made arrangements for food to be served to the Kalamukhas at numerous temples. And so, she was certain that the Kalamukhas would do her no harm. Why, they might even help her out. She knew that a mahasangam had been organised that day. She had seen several groups of Kalamukhas on her way from Pazhaiyarai to Kudandai. However, why were these men hiding behind the trees? What if they did not know she was from the Kodumbalur family? They might do her some harm in that case, might they not?

Even as these thoughts were running through her head, the men emerged from the trees and began to run forward. They surrounded the palanquin. And yet, she remained unperturbed. She would tell them who she was. But before she could form the words, two of them grabbed her maid and bound the girl to a tree. A terrified shriek escaped Vanathi's mouth. One of the Kalamukhas pointed his trishul at her and barked, 'Penne! Shut up now! If you don't make a sound, you won't come to any harm. If you do, I'll kill you with this trishul!'

Vanathi mustered up her courage and demanded, 'Do you know who I am? I am Kodumbalur Velaar's daughter. If you so much as touch me, you'll pay for it dearly!'

The daring she felt did not reach her voice, which shook as she spoke.

'We know everything. That's why we've been lying in wait for you. Now, shut up! Or else ...' the Kalamukha said, aiming his trishul.

At the same time, the sound of a whip lashing through the air, and screams of 'Aiyooo!' rent the air.

Vanathi realised the Kalamukhas must be whipping the palanquin bearers. Angered, she tried to get out of the palanquin. But she did not get the chance, for the palanquin bearers began to run. The Kalamukhas ran along with them, surrounding her ride. They shouted as they ran, and Vanathi realised there was no point in trying to outshout them. Neither would it be wise to jump off a fast-moving palanquin. And even if she jumped, she would land right in the midst of these terrifying men. Even as all this was happening, she couldn't help feeling curious about where they were taking her and why.

After they had run for about half a naazhigai, they arrived at an ancient Durga temple, nestled among the trees. The night was well and truly upon them by now. One of the Kalamukhas went inside the temple, from where he picked up the lamp that had been lit for the night. He brought it to the palanquin and held it up to Vanathi's face.

'Penne!' he said. 'We're going to ask you some questions. If you answer without fuss, we'll let you go without harming you. Or, we'll escort you wherever you want to go.'

A sudden suspicion popped into Vanathi's head.

'What do you think I know?' she asked. 'What are you going to ask me?'

'Penne! You're making this solitary journey for a secret meeting with someone, aren't you? Who is that? Whom are you going to meet in private?'

Vanathi's suspicions were confirmed. Now, she underwent a complete change. The doe that was scared by the slightest noise was transformed into a lioness that feared nothing at all.

'What concern is it of yours whom I meet? Who do you think you are to ask me such questions? I will not answer you!' Vanathi said.

The Kalamukha laughed. 'You don't have to tell us!' he said. 'We already know. You're going to meet Prince Arulmozhi Varman. Tell us where he's hiding. We'll let you go unharmed.'

'You can do whatever you want to me. But you won't learn a thing from me!' Vanathi snapped back.

'You say we can do whatever we want. If you knew what we intended to do, you wouldn't dare say such a thing!'

'What are you going to do? You might as well tell me.'

'Well, first, we'll bring one of your delicate hands to a torch and burn it until all the flesh turns to char. Then, we'll do the same to the other hand. Then, we'll bring the torch to your hair, and set it on fire.'

'Feel free to do that. Here's my hand! Bring the torch to me!' Vanathi said.

She was aware of the conspiracies and plans that were being plotted by the traitors in the empire. These men must be the conspirators' soldiers in disguise, she thought. They were trying to find out where the prince was. They intended to do him some harm, she was sure. If she was going to be tortured to death for refusing to reveal anything about the prince, well, so be it. What greater honour could there be than this fate? The thought gave her the courage she was seeking.

'Penne! Think before you speak. What's the point of such obstinacy? You'll regret it. Do you want to spend all your life as a blind woman?' the Kalamukha said.

'You can set fire to every atom of my being. You can cut my flesh into pieces. But you will not extract a word from me!' Vanathi said.

'Well then, we must go about our business. Shishya! Bring that torch here!' the Kalamukha said.

Vanathi was suddenly distracted by something a short distance away. She saw a procession of elephants and horses and soldiers and palanquins approaching them. By the grace of God, some unexpected help had turned up, she thought.

'Careful! Look there!' she said, pointing towards the approaching procession.

The Kalamukha laughed. 'Do you know who's coming?' he asked.

'It seems to be Prime Minister Aniruddhar. If I scream now, the people in the procession will hear me. Careful! Let me go, and run away. Or else ...'

'You're right, penne! It is indeed Prime Minister Anbil Aniruddhar. It is under his orders that we have captured you,' the Kalamukha said.

Fear took hold of Vanathi again. Another terrified scream made its way up her throat. She held her hands to her mouth to stifle it.

17

GAJENDRA MOKSHAM

All this time, Vanathi had remained in the palanquin. Now, the palanquin was set on the ground. Vanathi got out and stood, staring at the procession. The Kalamukhas looked on in silence too. The only sounds that broke this silence were the croaking of frogs and the rustling of leaves in the night breeze.

The idea of escape did not even occur to Vanathi. She knew it was impossible. Even if she got away from the Kalamukhas, she could not so much as dream of getting away from Aniruddha Brahmarayar. Everyone knew of his intelligence, shrewdness and cunning. It was also a known fact that he exercised great influence with the emperor. The women of the Pazhaiyarai palace would gossip about every other leader, minister and suzerain king, but would not speak a word about Aniruddha Brahmarayar. They knew that even a whispered word spoken in the farthest corners of the antapuram would somehow make its way to

Aniruddhar's ears. And the Chakravarti might forgive anything else, but he would not tolerate a slight against his dearest friend.

Vanathi, like everyone else, was aware of all this. Princess Kundavai Devi had the deepest respect for the prime minister. This was why Vanathi had expected that he would rescue her from these men. But the Kalamukha's claim that she had been captured at the prime minister's instance had disconcerted her.

Why would he issue such a command? She was an orphan, after all. What information could she have? Perhaps these men were lying? Perhaps it was the Pazhuvettaraiyar brothers' entourage that was approaching? Or even Madurantakar's? Whoever it was, she was certain of one thing. She would not reveal what she knew about the prince, no matter what they did to her. They could take her life, but they would not break her silence. The thought reignited her courage. Let them come, whoever it was! She would prove the bravery of the Kodumbalur clan. She would prove her worthiness as Princess Kundavai's friend and confidant.

A lone palanquin broke off from the procession. The elephants, the horses and the retinue stayed back. Once the palanquin had reached Vanathi, the bearers set it on the ground. The prime minister emerged from it.

At a sign from him, the palanquin bearers and Kalamukhas moved some distance away.

Aniruddhar looked Vanathi up and down and said, 'What a wonder! I'm not dreaming, am I? It *is* the Kodumbalur princess who stands before me, isn't it? It *is* the beloved daughter of the Eezham martyr Parantaka Siriya Velaar, isn't it?'

'Yes, indeed, aiya! And I'm not dreaming either, am I? The person standing before me *is* Anbil Aniruddha Brahmarayar, who commands the fear and respect of the entire Chozha empire, isn't it? It *is* the prime minister who is the Chakravarti's most trusted confidant, isn't it?' Vanathi said.

'Thaaye! I'm pleased that you know who I am. This makes my task easier. And I won't have to trouble you much either.'

'Oh, please don't worry on that account. Any trouble to which I'm put at the behest of such an iconic minister as yourself will not bother me. Why, I won't even consider it trouble!'

'Your words put my heart at rest. I don't intend to put you to much trouble either. I just have a couple of questions for you. As long as you answer them, you ...'

'Aiya! I have some questions for you, before you pose yours to me.'

'Do ask, amma! Ask away without hesitation. I am as a father to you. I consider you a daughter. I met your uncle at Mathottam some days ago. He told me I should care for you as a daughter. I assured him I would.'

'Vandanam, my father! Once upon a time, the Chakravarti promised he would be a father to me, having been rendered fatherless by the war in Eezham. And now, I've found another father in you. What could I possibly lack?'

'Ask me whatever you wanted to ask, amma, and quickly! The clouds are gathering. It could start pouring any moment.'

'O father! Was it you who asked these Kalamukhas to accost your beloved daughter, who was journeying on her palanquin, and bring her here by force? Was it also you who told them to burn this hapless, helpless girl's hands with the flame of a torch? These terrifying men made that accusation against you. But I didn't believe them.'

'My child! They were speaking the truth. It was indeed I who issued such a command. If that is wrong, I take full responsibility for it.'

'O prime minister of Chozha Naadu, famed in all three worlds! Your words surprise me. "If that is wrong", you say! You are well-versed in the scriptures, in dharma shastra and neethi shastra. It is you who are responsible for upholding law and order in Chozha Naadu. It is you who have been given the right to point it out if the Chakravarti himself were to err. If you don't know whether something is wrong or not, who else would? Would you say accosting a hapless, helpless woman travelling in a palanquin, bringing her somewhere by force and threatening to torture her is wrong? Or not? Who can tell if you cannot? I have heard that there is absolutely no danger on the roads under Sundara Chozha Chakravarti's rule. I have also heard that scoundrels who harm women will be punished with particular severity. If you don't know whether what happened to me is wrong or not, it is a matter of some surprise, is it not?'

Prime Minister Aniruddhar was stunned. He had made two futile attempts to interrupt Vanathi. Now, he said in a hard voice, 'Penne! Have some patience. Do not put your sophistry on display in its entirety, all at once! It is not without reason that I am in a dilemma about whether what happened to you was wrong or not. The answer will depend on your response to my question. I had heard that a woman who was in the know of a crucial royal secret was on the road to Nagapattinam. I asked my men to stop that woman. They did what they did with the intention of obeying my orders. They might have erred. They might have mistaken you, who was simply returning from the astrologer's house after consulting him, for the conspirator who was travelling on the same road. My daughter! Tell me! Was it your intention to return from Kudandai to Pazhaiyarai? Was it the palanquin bearers who made a mistake and took you down the wrong road, the one that leads to Nagapattinam? You weren't heading there to meet someone who was conspiring against the empire, were you? If you can prove you weren't, then what these men did to you was wrong. And I do have a part in it. What do you say, penne? Let me put this more bluntly. You were not heading to Nagapattinam to meet Prince Arulmozhi Varman in secret, were you?'

The princess was now flustered. She was so furious she wanted to grab the torch and set the prime minister on fire. But she knew there was little point in showing him how angry she was. Suddenly, the girl who was entirely clueless about disingenuity and dissembling turned into an astute politician who knew just how to measure her words.

Without answering the prime minister's question directly, she said, 'Aiya! What a thing to say! Is it your view that Prince Arulmozhi Varmar is conspiring against the empire? Isn't it wrong for you to speak thus about the emperor's beloved son? Why, isn't that itself treason to the Chozha clan? Aha! I must tell Kundavai Piraatti about this right away!'

'Oh, do feel free to do so, thaaye! If you will simply answer my question, we need not waste any more time here. I will escort you safely to Ilaiya Piraatti myself.'

'And if I refuse to answer ...?'

'You don't have that option, thaaye! It isn't that easy to escape from this old man, you see. You will simply *have* to answer my question,' the prime minister said.

'Aiya! Omnipotent Prime Minister Aniruddha Brahmarayare! You cannot possibly learn anything about the prince from this entirely impotent orphan girl. These scoundrels can burn my hands as they have threatened to do, but I won't speak a word.'

'O princess of the courageous Kodumbalur clan! I'm amazed by your intrepidness. But even while saying you wouldn't reveal a thing about the prince, you've made a revelation or two. If you will only tell me one more thing, it will make everything easier. What does it matter if you reveal a little more than you already have, anyway?'

Vanathi was flustered. Had she betrayed something by accident? The notion made her feel as if a cold fist was squeezing her heart. She thought over what she had said. No, there was no chance she had revealed anything. This old man was trying to trick her.

Bolstered by her certainty, she said, 'Aiya! How can such lies emerge from the very mouth that leads people in prayer? How can the prime minister of Sundara Chozhar make up something that isn't? I haven't said anything about the prince. And yet you claim I revealed something?'

'Give it some thought, thaaye. Think back to what you have said. If you think not speaking about something will preclude revealing details about it, you're in the wrong. I'm talking about what you let slip even without speaking. The entire world is in grief over the death of the prince at sea. The news has reached you too. And yet, you said you would not reveal a thing about the prince. What does that tell me? That you know the prince did not die at sea. When I said you were going to Nagapattinam to meet him, you did not deny it. You didn't ask me how you could possibly meet a dead man. You did not say you were going somewhere else and not Nagapattinam either. Therefore, you have already revealed that the prince is alive and in Nagapattinam, and that you are on your way to him. There are just two more details I need from you. Where exactly in Nagapattinam is the prince hiding? And how did you get to know about it? Once you answer these two questions, you won't have to endure a conversation with this old man anymore. You can go wherever you like.'

Vanathi's heart had practically stopped. She realised the prime minister was right. Her foolishness had given the prince away. How could she possibly make up for such a grievous error? There was simply no way. She would have to end her life, that was all.

'Aiya! You claimed to be a dear friend of my uncle's. You also elevated our relationship to that of father and daughter. I make a request of you. I wish to go neither to Nagapattinam nor to Pazhaiyarai ...'

'Then to Kodumbalur, I presume. Well, that's fair enough. I will have you sent there safely.'

'No, aiya, I don't wish to go to Kodumbalur either. I wish to leave this world and go to another. Would you ask your men to place me on that sacrificial slab there, and offer me as a sacrifice? I'm ready!' she said.

'Thaaye! I promised to send you wherever you wished to go. If you wish to cross over to another world, I'm happy to oblige. But you must answer those two questions before I do so.'

'Aiya, please don't torment me any further. I will not answer your questions. If what you said sometime earlier is true, about considering me a daughter ...'

'My daughter! There is no doubt on that account. I consider you my very own daughter, my daughter by birth. Perhaps you don't know just how close I am to your family. Your uncle and I have been friends for four decades. But where royal matters are concerned, one cannot be moved by kinship and friendship. Not even by parental and filial ties. Why, look at the case of the Chakravarti himself! The moment he learned his son was conspiring against the crown, did he not order him arrested and brought back?'

'Aiya! Are you saying these words about Ponniyin Selvar? What did he do for you to accuse him of conspiring against the crown?'

'Oho! It appears you genuinely don't know. Ponniyin Selvar went to Lanka claiming he was going to fight a war. Our army decimated the Lankan one. The prince tried to capitalise on the opportunity to claim the Lankan throne. Isn't that treason? The moment he heard about this, the emperor ordered his son arrested and brought to him. The prince flouted this order and jumped into the sea of his own volition to evade punishment; it was his intention that he should be presumed dead. Even as the rumours run wild, he has got ashore safely and is staying hidden somewhere. Perhaps you refused to reveal the exact spot where he's hiding because you didn't know the context. If you insist on sheltering such a traitor, it would be treason on your part. So, please do tell me, amma!' the prime minister said.

The rage Vanathi had been controlling thus far now came pouring out. She couldn't bear to hear the prince spoken of in this manner. The submissive girl now transformed into the very embodiment of strength, as she said, 'Aiya! There is no truth to a single thing you say! You have made terrible accusations against the prince, all untrue! When our armies were withering from exhaustion and disillusionment in Lanka, the prince's arrival inspired them and imbued them with a fresh lease of life! The entire world knows that the credit for our victories in Lanka goes entirely to Ponniyin Selvar. His bravery, generosity and various other wonderful qualities won the hearts of the Lankan people. They wished for him to take the place of their king, who had fled the battlefield and has been in hiding since. The Buddhist monks offered Ponniyin Selvar the Lankan throne and crown. But he turned them down. And here you are, making such awful accusations against a man of such integrity! When the prince was told the order to arrest him had come from his father, he surrendered right away and headed straight for Thanjai. He did not jump into the sea of his own volition for any reason but to save the life of his dear friend. He did not conspire against the emperor either. What sin must I have committed that my ears were fated to hear such horrible things about him!'

Aniruddhar said, with a little laugh, 'Penne! Do you know what people would think if they heard you defending Arulmozhi Varmar with such passion? That the two of you were lovers!'

'Aiya! There is some truth to what you have said. Half of it, to be precise. It is true that I have lost my heart to him. I don't wish to hide that from you. But it would not be right for him to make space in his heart for this orphan. The andril bird[1] may fall in love with the full moon glowing in the sky. But the moon cannot even know of the existence of such a bird, can it?'

'Aha! I was unaware until now that my dear friend's daughter was such an accomplished poet. Of course, you *are* Ilaiya Piraatti's dear friend!'

'Enough, enough. I don't wish to hear praise from you. Either let me go on my way, or call your men here and give them the order!'

'Penne! Have some patience! You know ever so much about Ponniyin Selvar. Clearly, you know where he is at this moment too. Tell me that one detail alone, and I will send you to your uncle right away. He is on his way back from Lanka. He must have reached Madurai by now.'

'Aiya! A man who can be friends with such an evil person as yourself is not qualified to be my uncle. I have no kith and no kin. I only told you what everyone knows about the prince. You will not learn anything more from me. There is no point in dragging this on anymore.'

'True, we must not drag this on. It appears there will be a tremendous downpour ...'

'Just a downpour? A place where people like you live will be subject to lightning strikes and thunderbolts and a deluge itself!'

As if to prove Vanathi's averment, a bolt of lightning tore through the sky, followed by a deafening roar of thunder that shook the very earth.

'Penne! So, you won't tell me where Prince Arulmozhi Varman is?'

'I won't!'

'So, it is as I thought. You're carrying some secret message to the prince's hiding spot. Is this true or not?'

'Aiya, there is no point in this. I don't intend to answer any further questions from you.'

'Well, in that case, I will have to accord you the punishment reserved for all those guilty of treason. There is no other option.'

'I wait in anticipation of this punishment, aiya! If my head must be lopped off on the sacrificial slab, I am happy to place my neck against its edge in preparation.'

'Chhe chhe! You're a princess of the Kodumbalur clan! Surely such a pedestrian punishment is unbefitting of you! Look, there, at that elephant!'

Vanathi looked in the direction he was pointing.

An enormous elephant loomed like a black mountain against the dark sky. As if to place the coal of the animal's skin in relief, two ivory tusks gleamed white in the moonlight.

'Penne! You have heard of Gajendra Moksham, have you not? When an elephant devoted to Lord Vishnu was trapped by a crocodile, who had latched on to one leg, the lord had rushed to the elephant's rescue. He killed the crocodile and granted moksham to the elephant, Gajendra. And this Gajendra you see before you has, in turn, granted moksham to countless traitors. You said you wanted to leave this world for another one, didn't you? The elephant will grant your wish in the blink of an eye. He will wrap you in his trunk and toss you right into that other world!'

With that, Aniruddha Brahmarayar laughed.

His laughter made Vanathi's hair stand on end. This was no man, she thought. He was a rakshasha in human form.

'Princess, I ask you once and for all, will you tell me where Ponniyin Selvan is? Or would you like to attain moksham by way of this elephant's trunk?'

The words gave Vanathi the strength she needed to ask, in a clear voice, 'Aiya! Will you call Gajendra to me? Or shall I go to Gajendra myself?'

Aniruddhar made a gesture with his hands. And then, he said something in a language Vanathi did not understand.

The elephant began to thunder towards them, and came to a stop at Vanathi's side. She felt the elephant's trunk curl around her slender body, and then felt her feet lift off the ground.

A series of thoughts and images flashed through Vanathi's mind in those few seconds. She was stunned by her own courage. Ilaiya Piraatti used to call her a coward and tease her about it all the time! If only Kundavai could have seen her now! Surely, she would get to hear of this somehow? She would get to hear of how Vanathi had sacrificed her life to protect Ponniyin Selvar? And Kundavai would tell her brother of it, for sure. What would the prince think of her then? Would he realise at least then that the princess of Kodumbalur was even braver than that boat-girl?

The elephant's trunk rose high into the air, carrying Vanathi with it.

Yes, yes, that Brahmarakshasha had not lied this time. The elephant was certainly going to grant her moksham. She would be tossed into the air in a moment. How far would she fly before she fell? But she would not be conscious when she hit the ground. She would be dead before she knew it.

Vanathi had now risen above the elephant's head. She closed her eyes. The elephant's trunk twisted once in the air, as if about to toss her away. Fortunately for Vanathi, she lost consciousness at that very moment.

18

ANAIMANGALAM

So, Vanathi who is one of our heroines has this habit of fainting every now and again, doesn't she? We ask that our readers bear with it this one time. Because, soon enough, she'll be cured of this ailment.

When Vanathi came to, at first she felt like she was sitting on a swing. Then, she had the sense she was flying through the air. She could hear the pleasant 'rim-rim', 'jhim-jhim' of raindrops and feel the 'gup-gup' of the cool night breeze. Her body shivered slightly. She must be travelling through the skies to the heavens, she thought. It was dark around her, but lightning flashed every now and again.

She had a vague memory of the prime minister speaking of Gajendra moksham, and the elephant's trunk curling around her waist.

So, it was as the prime minister had said. Her life in the world of humans had ended, and she was going to her celestial abode. She had attained moksha, and would soon meet the devas and apsaras.

But she would not see *him*, her own lord and master, the man she had taken for a husband in her own heart ... what joy could there be in an eternity without the love of one's life?

What was this? Her body seemed to be swinging wildly, but her head was resting against something soft, something as comforting as a mother's lap. Why, it felt like the lap of the woman who had showered her with more love than a mother could, Ilaiya Piraatti! Aaah ... what was Kundavai Devi doing in Pazhaiyarai now, she wondered. Would the news of her beloved friend's death have reached the princess?

Right, so Vanathi knew she was travelling through the skies to the heavens. But what vehicle was carrying her there? Was it the Pushpak Vimaan? Or was it Indra's elephant Airavata? Oh, no, she would not think of elephants now. The very thought of the animal filled her with fear. Elephants and their twisting, curling trunks! How much strength that trunk had! Well, it was all over anyway. She was dead. What was the point of fearing anything?

But what was that soft, soft pillow against which her head was resting? She could not see in the dark. She would feel with her hands, though. It felt like silk. It *was* silk. And it was rather wet.

Aha! What was this? Someone was caressing her cheeks with fingers as delicate as jasmine flowers ...

'Vanathi! Vanathi!'

'Akka? Is it really you?'

'Of course. Who else could it be?'

'Are you coming to Mokshalokam with me?'

'Why are you in such a hurry to go to Mokshalokam? Are you already so tired of this world?'

'Then, where are we going?'

'Have you forgotten this too? Don't you know we're headed to Anaimangalam?'

'What? Where? Tell me the name of the place again?'

'What a girl! Anaimangalam. That's where we're going. We're journeying there by elephant.'

'Aiyo! Did you say "elephant"?'

'You crazy girl! Why are you trembling? Have you begun to fear elephants, on top of everything else, now?'

'Akka! Did I fall asleep at some point?'

'Yes, yes. Soon after we got on the howdah, you were soothed into sleep by the rocking motion!'

'Nothing soothing about it, Akka! I had a terrible nightmare!'

'That's what it sounded like. You were blabbering all sorts of nonsense.'

'What did I blabber, Akka?'

'You spoke of Kalamukhas. Then you spoke of human sacrifices. Then you said something about Gajendra moksham. And elephant trunks. Then, you started cursing the prime minister, calling him a "paavi" and a "traitor". Not that he doesn't deserve it! If he were to hear what you said in your sleep, he wouldn't be able to sleep for days on end!'

'Was all that really a dream, Akka?'

'A real dream? Or an unreal dream? What do I know? I don't even know what your dream was about!'

'The Kalamukhas waylaid me and took me captive. The prime minister began to interrogate me about the prince. Then, he ordered an elephant to be brought there. I was to be tossed into the air and killed by the elephant. I did not waver, Akka. I stayed strong. I thought of you, and wished you could have been there to see how brave I was!'

'Well, you were able to stay courageous at least in a dream! I'm happy for it!'

Vanathi was silent for a while, and then said, 'I'm not able to bring myself to believe it.'

'To believe what?'

'That it was all a dream.'

'Sometimes, dreams can seem that way. They seem all too real. I've had such vivid dreams too.'

'What was your dream about? Tell me!'

'Why, I dream of my brother all the time! It's been months since he went to Lanka. But the moment I close my eyes, he appears in the flesh before me.'

'How lucky you are, Akka!'

'Humph! Only you can speak of my luck! How would you know how heartbroken I've been, how much every part of me has been hurting, since news reached me of my brother having drowned at sea!'

'You're saying that was not part of the nightmare? Is that part alone true, of his having drowned at sea?'

'If only that had been a nightmare! But, no, that part alone is true, Vanathi! An eyewitness told me of his having jumped into the sea. How can I refuse to believe it?'

'You're talking about our Vaanar warrior, aren't you? But didn't he say something else about the prince? About a boat-girl and the Nagapattinam Choodamani Vihara?'

'You must have dreamt all this. Oh, yes, you were mumbling about a boat-girl called Poonguzhali, and about the Choodamani Vihara in your sleep. You also said something about how you intended to join the Buddhist order and become a bhikshuni. Why are you so disillusioned with this earthly life? Why do you want to renounce it all?'

'Akka! Don't you know? Have I not opened my heart to you? When the sea has swept him away, what life do I have left? If only it hadn't been a dream ... if only the elephant had truly hurled me to my death!'

'Adi, paavi! What would become of me if I lost you too?'

'It's different for you, Akka. You ...'

'True, true. Arulmozhi is dearer to you than he is to me! That's how it is, isn't it?'

'Akka, that's not what I'm saying. I don't have the strength of mind and heart that you do. Now that he's dead ...'

'Chhi, chhi! What a thing to say! Why must you say he's dead? Are you sure of such a thing?

Pazhuvettaraiyar and Pazhuvoor Rani and that moron Madurantakan will go on about it and announce it to everyone. But why should you and I join the chorus? Why should we even think such a thing has happened?'

'What are you saying, then? That he could have survived the storm? How? How does one jump into the sea in the middle of a tempest and survive? And if he had, would he not have turned up by now?'

'You crazy girl! He jumped into the sea, but does that mean he drowned?'

'If he had reached the shore safely, surely we'd have heard about it by now?'

'Do you know what happened to my father? He went missing for several months in Lanka. They eventually found him and crowned him prince. My grandfather Arinjaya Chozhar went missing for *years* after the war at Takkolam. He was eventually found, alive and well. Now, listen to me, Vanathi! Kaveri Amman once saved my brother from drowning. Now, it is Samudra Raja's turn. Ponniyin Selvan would have reached the shore safely. Numerous little islands dot the sea between our coastline and that of Lanka. Arulmozhi Varman could be on any of those, couldn't he? I've undertaken this journey to ensure that they search thoroughly. And I brought you along. Don't you remember the conversation we had about this? Well, I don't blame you. Ever since news of the prince has arrived, you have completely lost your senses. You've just about begun to speak coherently!'

Vanathi was silent for a while. Then, she said, 'Akka! Where did you say we were going?'

'To Anaimangalam.'

'And where is that?'

'Near Nagapattinam, by the shore. The Choodamani Vihara you were going on about is not far from Anaimangalam. If you do intend to join the Buddhist order, it would be quite convenient for you too. But don't be in a hurry to follow in Manimeghalai's footsteps. Let's wait for confirmation about Ponniyin Selvan before you jump into anything!' Ilaiya Piraatti said, and laughed.

'Akka! You're laughing! How are you able to bring yourself to laugh? Are you so very sure that the prince has survived?'

'If I did not have faith that he is alive, could I even function, Vanathi? His horoscope cannot be false. The predictions of all the astrologers cannot be false. The conch and discus marks on his palms cannot be false! Everything is going as it should.'

'What is going as it should? I don't understand a thing,' Vanathi said.

'Why would you? You're delirious and delusional. How could you possibly understand? The astrologer said Arulmozhi would face all sorts of dangers and obstacles in his youth. That has come to pass. That means everything else will come true too!'

'What do you mean by "everything else"?'

'How many times should I tell you? How many times have you heard this before? Why do you ask again? Now, go to sleep. Let's talk in the morning.'

Vanathi immersed herself in silent contemplation for a time, and then said, 'Is this elephant ride going to stretch on through the night? Why?'

'Do you not remember even this? If we travel by day, people will surround us. They will ask where Ponniyin Selvan is, where Chozha Naadu's beloved son is, what has become of him ... they will accuse the Pazhuvettaraiyar brothers and curse the Pazhuvoor Rani. They might even blame the emperor. Why should we put ourselves through all this? And who knows, the Pazhuvettaraiyar brothers might well accuse me of instigating the subjects of this empire against them! I decided to travel by night so we might avoid all this trouble. I told you all this even as we were preparing for the journey in Pazhaiyarai! And now you ask me again! Clearly, you're not yourself. We must ask the monks at the Choodamani Vihara to cure you of whatever is ailing your mind. We'll see about all that later. Now, go to sleep! I'm feeling drowsy myself. This moving mountain will be our bed for the night!'

Vanathi decided she would not speak anymore. Her mind was in turmoil. She played back the events of the evening in her mind. They seemed too real to be part of a dream. She was fine, she thought to herself. It was Ilaiya Piraatti who was trying to make her lose her mind. She tried to remember what had happened after the elephant had hoisted her up into the air. But she couldn't recall a thing.

Well, what could have happened? Her akka must have turned up at that very moment and saved her life, that's what! And the moment the princess appeared, the prime minister must have trembled with fear. Even so, how could Kundavai Devi have saved her from the clutches of an elephant?

But, then ... there was another possibility. Perhaps the elephant they were riding on was the very animal that had hoisted her up ... She had seen a howdah on that elephant's back. Even in the dark, the silhouette of the howdah had stood out. Ilaiya Piraatti must have been seated inside. The elephant had not tossed her into the air, but placed her gently inside the howdah. She had seen the trained palace elephants do this several times. Had the prime minister and princess conspired to do this? Why, though? Clearly, to stop her from journeying all alone to Nagapattinam. And perhaps to put her courage to the test. It was Ilaiya Piraatti who had once arranged for a fake crocodile to scare her, wasn't it? Well, whatever it was, she realised it had been a mistake to set off on her own. How comforting it was to lie with her head on her akka's lap! How wonderfully her akka's words had bolstered her confidence and faith! Ponniyin Selvan must be safe somewhere. Yes, without doubt! Perhaps this journey would end in their meeting him? The thought made Vanathi's heart leap with joy. The disillusionment she had felt earlier was now transformed into anticipation.

The elephant was striding along. The howdah rocked gently with each movement. Soldiers marched before and behind them. The rain petered out into a drizzle, and soon the drizzle faded too. The clouds parted, and stars peeped out from behind them.

Vanathi looked at the stars through the roof of the howdah. She wondered whether there could possibly be a connection between the stars in the sky and the lives people led on this Earth. Could the star under which Ponniyin Selvar was born truly be compatible with the one under which she was born, as the astrologer had said? Was there such a thing as compatibility between stars? Could it be true that she would birth a son who would rule the entire world? People said the appearance of a shooting star was ominous. Could that be true? If it was indeed a bad omen, what did it portend? Was it the drowning of Ponniyin Selvar? Or would he return, as her akka believed? In that case, what did the shooting star portend?

These thoughts troubled Vanathi for a long time. Then, her eyelids began to feel heavy. When she opened her eyes again, it was light outside. The birds were chirping merrily. Ilaiya Piraatti was awake too.

As Vanathi rose, Kundavai Devi parted the curtain and said, 'Ah, here we are! We've reached Anaimangalam. We've reached the Chozha palace here.'

The elephant came to standstill and then sat on its haunches so the princesses could descend.

They entered the Chozha palace, where maids were waiting for them. They showed the princesses around the palace, and eventually led them to the garden, from where they could see a stream that led to the sea.

As they stood watching, Vanathi asked, 'Akka! You said you were going to make arrangements to find the prince? What have you done?'

'Yes, Vanathi! Arrangements have already been made. Look, there's a boat approaching us. Perhaps the people rowing it are bringing us some news!' Kundavai said.

Vanathi looked. A boat appeared through the branches of the trees along the shore. It had two occupants.

'Akka, who is on the boat?' she asked.

'The man rowing the boat is Senthan Amudan. Remember, we released him from the Thanjavur dungeon. The woman sitting by his side is Poonguzhali.'

Vanathi's hair stood on end. 'Akka! I don't wish to meet that girl. I will be inside the palace,' she said, and turned to leave.

'Why are you so scared of her? Is she going to eat you alive? I'm right here. You stay, now!' Kundavai said.

As the boat approaches the two women, we use the opportunity to fill our readers in on what really happened. How did Vanathi escape the elephant's clutches? Well, her second guess was right. The elephant had not tossed her into the air, but placed her inside the howdah, where Kundavai Devi was waiting to receive her, hidden behind a curtain. The princess had placed her friend's unconscious head on her lap.

The prime minister had seated himself in his palanquin and said, 'Devi, I'll take your leave. May your journey be pleasant! And may it end in joy!'

'Aiya, thank you ever so much for your help!' Ilaiya Piraatti said.

'You said the Kodumbalur princess was a coward, didn't you? I have never met as steadfast a woman as she!'

'She used to be a coward. But things have changed recently,' Kundavai said.

'That change is due to you. That girl must think I'm a horrible rakshasha. Well, that's as it may be. The world is full of people with various opinions about me. What's one more? Go well, amma!'

Once the prime minister had taken his leave, his palanquin and its escort of four soldiers headed west, while the elephant with its procession of horses and soldiers went east.

Not long after they had parted ways, it began to pour. The prime minister's palanquin bearers and bodyguards sped through the rain, not allowing it to slow them down one bit. But as the rain let up, they came to a sudden halt.

'Why have you stopped?' the prime minister asked.

'Swami, someone appears to be lying under that tree!' a soldier at the head of their procession said.

The prime minister squinted in the direction the man was pointing.

A bolt of lightning flashed at that very moment.

'Yes, I can see a man lying there. Let me go and have a look,' the prime minister said.

He stepped out of the palanquin and approached the man, who was mumbling something.

'Who goes there?' Aniruddhar said.

A frail voice said, 'That sounds like the prime minister ...'

'Yes, I *am* the prime minister. Who are you?'

'Aiya! Don't you recognise me? I'm Madurantakan!'

'Ilavarase! What is this! How did you get here? What happened?' the prime minister cried, and rushed forward to help Madurantakar to his feet.

19

MADURANTAKAN'S GRATITUDE

The moment the prime minister touched Madurantakan, the prince began to wail.

'Aiyo! Appa! I'm dead! Don't touch me! My legs! My legs! They're gone! It's all over!'

Aniruddhar paused in his attempt to lift the prince and asked anxiously, 'Ilavarase! What happened to you? What's become of your legs?'

'My legs are broken! I cannot walk. I cannot even stand.'

The prime minister turned to the servants and said, 'Ade! Bring the palanquin here!'

Then, he asked Madurantakan, 'Aiya, how did you get into such an accident? Why are you lying like this, all alone in the rain? Where is your entourage? How dare they leave you like this? No punishment would suffice for this abrogation of duty!'

'Prime Minister! There is no call for punishment. No one is guilty of abrogating one's duty. It was I who set off on a horse all by myself in the evening. I was riding along the river bank. All of a sudden, it began to rain. A bolt of lightning and a clash of thunder frightened my horse, who reared up and ran away. I was thrown off when he ran past this tree, for I hit one of its branches. I don't know where the horse is. I don't know whether my leg is broken or simply sprained from the impact of the fall. I'm not able to stand. It's a good thing you happened to pass this way at this time.'

'It must be all the good deeds your great father, that icon of Shiva bhakti Kandaraditya Devar, wrought, that such a happy coincidence occurred. Now that I'm here, you needn't worry. Please grit your teeth and bear the pain. I'll have you shifted to the palanquin. We can talk later, once we reach my home in Nadankoil.'

The palanquin was brought close, and the prime minister gently carried the prince to it and placed him inside. He asked the bearers to carry the palanquin carefully, making sure the prince was not tossed about too much. He walked by the side of the palanquin.

It was not long before they arrived at the Sundara Chozha Vinnagaram, which was also known as Nadankoil. One of the mansions allocated to the prime minister was near the town temple. The men carried Madurantakar to the bedroom, and laid him on the bed. Aniruddha Brahmarayar examined his leg, and told him it wasn't broken. The fall had caused a sprain, which would ease up soon enough.

The prince had calmed down too.

Both men ate the prasadam, which had arrived from the temple for the prime minister.

Then, the prime minister said, 'Ilavarase! Do take rest tonight. Once day breaks, I'll arrange for your transport to wherever you wish to go. I'm going to Thanjai too. If you're happy to accompany me, it would be my honour and pleasure to escort you there.'

'Aiya, you have done me much ill in the past. But you've made up for all that today. I will never forget the help you've given me today. I will always be indebted to you, and I hope I will someday be able to prove how grateful I am. If things should pan out so that I ascend the Chozha throne, I will retain you as the prime minister!' Madurantakan said.

Aniruddhar made as if he was taken aback, and said, 'Ilavarase! I am indebted to the Chozha clan. It is my duty to advise or counsel anyone of this clan who should need it, and help out in any way I can. So, there is no need for you to make a gesture in gratitude to me, for you are a member of this clan. But ... you mentioned that I have done you ill in the past ... I'm afraid I don't understand. I don't remember having done you ill intentionally, but perhaps I have done so inadvertently? If you would be so kind as to tell me what my crime was, I will do whatever penance I must and make up for it in any way I can.'

'Aiya, Aniruddhare! It is common knowledge that you are extremely clever, intelligent and an expert at rajatantram[1]. But please don't flaunt your cunning with me. Please don't assume I don't know just what a terrible fate you had intended for me, what an evil turn you did me. Even so, in consideration of the timely help you gave me today, I am going to forgive and forget it all. If you can think of any way in which I can express my gratitude to you, please let me know. Is there a return favour I can do you?'

Aniruddhar smiled and said, 'Yes, ilavarase. There *is* one thing you can do as an expression of your gratitude. There is a request this old man begs to put to you. In the future, please don't ever set off alone on a horse as you did today. Please ride in a carriage, with guards before and behind you. Even better, go in a palanquin! These are tricky times. People are angry and frustrated for various reasons. You saw for yourself in Pazhaiyarai! So, perhaps it would be a better idea to choose a closed palanquin rather than an open one. And if you could get hold of the Pazhuvoor Ilaiya Rani's palanquin, it would be fantastic! Not a soul could suspect it is you behind the curtains!'

Madurantakan was stunned. His face betrayed his fear for a moment, but then he pulled himself together and said, 'Prime Minister! What a thing to say! What do you mean by asking me to travel in the Pazhuvoor Ilaiya Rani's palanquin? Is it your intention to humiliate me?'

'Ilavarase! I was not aware that you considered it humiliating to travel by the Pazhuvoor Ilaiya Rani's palanquin. Since when have you been nursing such a notion? Why, you used to journey in this manner quite regularly earlier! You must have had a change of heart after you returned from the Kadambur palace. An excellent decision, of course.'

Madurantakan was caught off guard. His face grew pale and he stuttered, 'Prime Minister! The Kadambur palace was not … I … I … didn't … I mean …'

'Ilavarase! You had gone to the Kadambur palace on the eighteenth day of the month of Adi with Dhanadhikari Periya Pazhuvettaraiyar, hadn't you? I was referring to that journey. You went and returned in the Ilaiya Rani's palanquin. I wasn't too pleased about it, truth be told. Palanquins should be used by men only when they're old and infirm, like me. Young men such as yourself should go by elephant or horse. But, of course, one needs to train in horse riding. Once your leg has healed, I will make arrangements for lessons myself, and …'

'Anbil Aniruddhare! Watch yourself. You're trying to humiliate me yet again! Just because one unfortunate incident has occurred, you've arrived at the conclusion that I don't know how to ride a horse. And just because I happened to journey in a palanquin once, you've decided that it is my wont to travel in the closed palanquin of the Pazhuvoor Rani. I'm doing my best to be tolerant, in view of your advanced age and the help you gave me today, but …'

'Ilavarase! Your tolerant attitude pleases me greatly. There is an old proverb which goes *Poruththaar bhoomi aalvaar*—*The tolerant will rule the entire world.* And what has Tamizhagam's greatest poet said?

Agazhvaarai thaangum nilam pola thammai
Igazhvaar poruththal thalai

As land bears with tolerance those who excavate it,
One must treat those who humiliate one.[2]

'The land not only *bears* but also *rewards* those who excavate it, with cool water. Those who hope to rule over lands must have this particular quality of the land. If an old man such as me should say something inappropriate, it would be prudent for you, who wish to rule the world, to tolerate it.'

'Aiya! Are you accusing me of wanting to rule the Chozha empire?' Madurantakan demanded. His lips twitched, his brows were knitted into a scowl. His fear had transformed into anger and frustration.

However, the prime minister responded in the same, unruffled voice, 'Ilavarase! Why do you say I'm accusing you? How is your desire to rule the Chozha empire in any way wrong? You are a descendant of that hero among warriors, Vijayalaya Chozhar. You are the son of the great Shiva devotee Kandaraditya Devar. You have every right to claim the Chozha throne. Why would I accuse you of wrongdoing if you wished to claim that right? And since it is not wrong, there is no need for subterfuge. If someone were to instigate you to enter into secret conspiracies in order to assert your right, please do not fall into that person's trap. Please lend this old man your ears for some time. Your parents wanted you to grow up in a certain way. You took to the worship of Shiva as they had hoped you would. Now, you have had a change of heart. No one has the right to fault this. You may make your appeal openly. You can speak to the Chakravarti himself about this. There is no need to go all alone to the Kollidam river on an Ammavaasai[3] night to meet, of all people, the chieftain of the Kalamukhas for aid. Or, to have a midnight conference at the Sambuvarayar palace like a meeting of thieves. Please understand that whoever made these suggestions to you does not have your best interests at heart. In fact, you must treat that person as your worst enemy.'

Madurantakan was caught in a dilemma. He couldn't believe the prime minister knew every detail of the secret meetings they had so carefully organised. At the same time, he felt, ever more oppressively, a sense of fear.

'Aiya! How did you learn all this? Which traitor pretended to be my friend only to betray me to you?' he asked.

'There is little point in your trying to find out. I have eyes on every wall and ears in every nook. Nothing can occur in this land without my learning of it.'

'Does that mean that the Chakravarti knows of all this too?' Madurantakan asked.

'No, he doesn't. Much that my eyes see and that my ears hear remains close to my chest. It is only when the need arises that I speak of things I have seen and heard.'

'True, true. There are some quite horrible secrets in your heart, eh? If those were to tumble out, won't that send a tremor through the Chozha empire?' Madurantakan said, his voice carrying a spiteful, even threatening, note for the first time.

Aniruddhar continued, as if he hadn't noticed, 'The emperor is a dear friend of mine. And yet I hold in my heart secrets that even he does not know. Sundara Chozhar is in his sickbed. For various reasons, he is already deeply hurt. I had no desire to further wound him by telling him of the conspiracy his suzerain kings have hatched. And there was no need for him to know. You may trust that I will not tell him what I know of your activities.'

'Aiya! Anbil Aniruddhare! Why are you suddenly so very concerned for the well-being of this idiot Madurantakan?' the prince asked with a sarcastic laugh.

'Ilavarase! My concern for your well-being is not sudden. Just as I do for Sundara Chozhar's children, I care for you too, immensely. It's just that I did not find the opportunity to show you that I ...'

'Oh, you found the opportunity today! It was quite opportune that I fell off my horse and broke my leg. Yet, there was a time when you would have broken my neck right there and gone on your way.'

'Narayana, Narayana! What are you saying, ilavarase?'

'Aiya! Please don't think I'm in the dark. Please don't think me such a fool as to believe just about anything I'm told. You began to conspire against me when I was still in my mother's womb. The moment I was born, you made arrangements for me to be killed. There, your face betrays your surprise. You're wondering how I know all this, aren't you? You think you're the only one who knows the terrible secrets hidden in Chozha Naadu, don't you?'

Now, Aniruddha Brahmarayar's face genuinely wore a perplexed expression. A series of emotions played across it. Finally, he forced a smile and said, 'Ilavarase! You're right, I did take pride in knowing some terrible secrets that I have not revealed to anyone else. Today, I see that was arrogance. Well, if I had made arrangements for your infanticide, how did you get out of it alive? Would you be so kind as to tell me that too?'

'It appears you want to test how much I know. Well, then. I'm happy to tell you. The men you had commissioned with the infanticide took the newborn baby without so much as checking whether it was a boy or girl. When they realised it was a girl, they came running to tell you. You took pity on the baby, decided it would do no harm to let a girl child live and handed her over to the temple priest for him to raise as his child. But within half a naazhigai of the girl's birth, I was born. You had not expected this twist in the tale. I must have been born under a lucky star, for I escaped. Even after the failure of your plot, you did your best to ensure I would not claim the throne. You arranged for me to be raised as a Shiva devotee, which is to say, a madman. This too failed. I didn't go entirely insane, as you'd hoped I would. Aiya! O Prime Minister! Why do you look so stunned? Why don't you swear that none of this is true?'

The prime minister was indeed stunned. Once he regained his power of speech, he said, 'Ilavarase! When you know all the details, what is the point of my trying to deny your charge? How would you believe me even if I swore that none of this is true?'

'You're right. There is no point! I know the reason for your sudden concern for me too. You don't like Aditya Karikalan. You had hoped Arulmozhi Varman would ascend the Chozha throne. Now that he has drowned at sea, you have turned to me. Yet, I promise you that I have forgiven and forgotten the ill you have wrought me. I will certainly reward you for the help you extended me today. If you'll be on my side from here on out, the moment I ascend the throne, I will retain you as my prime minister!'

'Ilavarase! Your words give me gooseflesh,' Aniruddha Brahmarayar said.

20

WHEN THE FEVER BROKE

Ponniyin Selvan was lying on a wooden cot in the room next to the quarters of the Acharya Bhikshu of the Nagapattinam Choodamani Vihara. He had been burning with fever for three days. Through most of it, he had been either asleep or delirious. The monks cared for him tirelessly, administering medication at particular hours and gently getting him to sip water so he would stay hydrated.

On the rare occasion that the prince woke with a clear head, he tried to figure out where he was. The painting on the wall facing him captivated the prince. Devas, Gandharvas and Yakshas had been depicted in the painting, some playing musical instruments, some bearing regal umbrellas and white chamaras—fly whisks intended for royal use—and others bearing golden plates with flowers of various hues blossoming in water. The figures were so lifelike that Ponniyin Selvan wondered if he had actually died and arrived in

Devalokam. The procession had assembled to welcome him, he thought.

How had he got here? He remembered travelling through a canal with thick shrub on either side, thazhampoo flowers peeking out from the leaves. The smell of thazhampoo teased his nostrils when he thought back to that journey. Had the boat carried him to the heavens? A young deva and an apsara had carried him off the boat, on a wooden plank. Yes, he remembered those two well. The deva must have been a Shiva devotee, for he sang verses from the Devaram. And the apsara? She did not sing. She spoke the odd word or two, but her voice was music in itself. He remembered her eyes, filled with affection and anxiety, staring at his face every time he had woken. Where were they now?

It appeared that aside from devas, Yakshas and Kinnars, Buddhist monks played important roles in Devalokam! He had not expected the bhikshus to be present in Devalokam, but from what he could tell, they were the guardians of the nectar. They approached him often, feeding him a few drops of nectar every time. For all the other luxuries Devalokam offered, there was no provision to slake one's thirst. His throat felt parched all the time, and the monks were stingy with the nectar. Why such miserliness in Devalokam, he wondered.

Well, perhaps too much nectar drunk all at once might have side effects? Was the drink they offered even nectar? Or some sort of intoxicant? Chhi, chhi ... would monks so much as *touch* an intoxicant, let alone administer it to a guest? But if the drink was nectar and not an intoxicant, why did he feel drowsy all the time? Not just drowsy, he felt drunk ... nectar was not supposed to make one sink into stupor, surely?

Ponniyin Selvan spent three days tormented by this confusion, and then woke up on the fourth, rid of the brain fog. He felt fresh, as if he had woken from a good night's rest. His body felt weak, but his mind was clear. He could see that the figures before him were part of a painting. And the Devas, Gandharvas, Yakshas and Kinnars were not welcoming him, but rather the Buddha, who had ascended to Devalokam. On another wall was a painting of the Buddha appearing in a dark sky, surrounded by clouds, a halo glowing behind him. Ah, he was in a Buddhist vihara, then. Which one, though? He began to remember everything that had transpired since he had begun his journey from Lanka. The last clear memory he had was of him and Vandiyadevan trying to stay afloat in the stormy sea.

At that moment, a bhikshu entered the room. He had a cup of nectar with him as usual. When he approached the prince, the monk stopped and took a careful look at him. The prince reached out for the cup and studied the liquid inside. It certainly was not nectar. It was some sort of medicine, or milk into which medicine had been ground.

The prince looked at the monk and asked, 'Swami, where am I? Who are you? How long have I been lying here like this?'

The monk did not answer his question. Instead, he turned and left the room.

The prince saw him hurry into the next room and heard him say, 'Acharya! The fever has broken. His clarity has returned!'

Soon after, an elderly monk entered the room. He approached the cot on which the prince was now sitting up, and studied him. Then, the monk smiled and said, 'Ponniyin Selva! You are at the Nagapattinam Choodamani Vihara! It has been three days since you arrived, plagued by a terrible fever. We are blessed to have had the opportunity to serve you and nurse you back to health!'

'And I'm blessed too. I have been longing to come see the Choodamani Vihara, of which I caught sight long ago, while passing by this port. The gods have smiled upon me, and seen to it that I had the fortune of staying here for a few days. But ... Swami, how did I get here? Do you know?'

'Ilavarase, please have the medicine first, and then I'll tell you everything I know,' the Acharya Bhikshu said.

The prince downed the contents of the cup and said, 'Aiya, this is not medicine. It is the nectar of the devas. You have put yourself to great trouble to cure me. But I will not thank you for it.'

The Acharya Bhikshu smiled and said, 'You don't need to thank us, ilavarase. Our religion believes it is man's first and foremost duty to help those who are ill. Why, our God has commanded that we nurse even sick and hurt animals back to health. It was no trouble at all caring for you. We are much obliged to the Chozha empire. Your father Sundara Chozha Chakravarti and your sister Ilaiya Piraatti have been great patrons of our religion. We are also aware that you yourself ordered the renovation of the Buddhist viharas in Anuradhapura. How could we expect you to thank us for this little return favour we have done you?'

'Acharya! When I said I wouldn't thank you, I did not mean it in that sense. I know just how dangerous the fever I had was ... I've seen men die like flies from this very fever in Lanka. I ought to have by rights reached Devalokam by now. Devas, Yakshas, Gandharvas and Kinnars would have assembled to welcome me as they do in that painting. I would have had the privilege of sitting among devas and apsaras and drinking the nectar of Devalokam! What a blissful life that would have been! And you've ruined it all for me, pulling me back from the very gates of Devalokam and bringing me to this world, with all its sorrows and troubles. So, I don't consider this a favour at all. And that is why I will not thank you for it.'

The Acharya Bhikshu's face broke into a smile. 'Ponniyin Selva! When the time comes for you to ascend to Devalokam, Indra will lead the devas down to this world himself and escort you in a grand procession. But that day is very far away. You have much to do in this world. Surely, you cannot think of going to Devalokam without completing your duties here!'

Ponniyin Selvan, who had been reclining against the backrest of the cot now sat up straight and looked at the Acharya Bhikshu. The prince's face was radiant, and his eyes glowed. To the monk, it seemed as if tiny bolts of lightning shot from the dark pupils of Arulmozhi Varman's large eyes, filling the room with beams.

'Acharya!' the prince said. 'You are right. I do wish to achieve certain things in this world. There are indeed duties I must carry out. I've seen the Choodamani Vihara from outside once. I've seen the stupas and viharas of Anuradhapuram. I am going to commission the expansion of the Choodamani Vihara so it becomes as large as the Abhayagiri Vihara of Anuradhapuram. And this vihara will have statues of the Buddha, enormous statues like those I saw at Abhayagiri. And the Shiva temples of Chozha Naadu must be renovated too. When I saw the awe-inspiring stupas and viharas in Lanka, I thought back to the tiny temples we have in this land and was embarrassed. The Thanjavur temple must have a gopuram that grazes the sky! And a statue of Mahadeva that is nearly as high! I will commission those. Acharya! The Buddhist stupas and Shiva temples of Chozha Naadu will compete with each other for height as they rise into the clouds. They will stand thousands of years, and everyone who gazes upon them will be stunned by the sight ...'

Having made this frenzied speech like a man possessed, the prince suddenly ran out of strength and began to lean back. The Acharya Bhikshu hurried forward to hold his head before it hit the backrest, and gently laid him down.

Stroking the prince's forehead, the monk said, 'Ilavarase! The visions you spoke of will be realised in time. But first, your body must heal. Please rest awhile.'

21

THE NANDI MANDAPAM

The Acharya Bhikshu returned to the prince's room the next afternoon.

Ponniyin Selvan was bursting with questions for the monk.

He had tried asking the junior monk who brought him his medicines and food, but the only response he had got was, 'Aiya! Gurudeva will tell you everything himself.'

When the Acharya Bhikshu eventually came in, the first thing he said to the prince was, 'Ilavarase! How are you feeling today?'

'I'm being assaulted from all sides, aiya! My brain demands, "Why are you lazing about? Get up! Run! Mount your horse! Jump into the river and swim! Wrestle down an elephant! Do something, anything, stop lying down all the time!" And my stomach won't stop complaining. The food your shishya brings is not enough, it says. Acharya! I can't believe I was ever ill.

Your medicine has worked such wonders!' Ponniyin Selvan said.

'Aiya! You must not pay too much heed to a brain that has just recovered. One feels a rush of energy right after recovery, but if you're careless now, you will have a relapse, and then we can do nothing at all to save you. It could pose mortal danger.'

'Gurudeva! I'm not worried about mortal danger ...'

'You're not, but the millions of people who populate Chozha Naadu have been driven to despair in the last few days ... everyone from the smallest child to the eldest man has been drowning in tears ...'

'Aiya! I don't understand what you're talking about. Why are the people of Chozha Naadu so worried? Did they think I would not recover from this fever? Why should they think I was in any danger when they know I'm in your care?'

'Ilavarase! The people are not aware that you were struck by fever, or that you are in the Choodamani Vihara, for that matter. If they knew, do you think this place would be so quiet? They would have broken down the walls in their eagerness to see you, wouldn't they? When news came of your having drowned at sea, you should have heard the wails of the people of this town ... why, there was not one dry eye in this vihara!'

Ponniyin Selvan sat up and said, 'Gurudeva! What are you talking about? I can make no sense of it at all! News came of my having drowned at sea? When? And who brought this news? Why?'

'I don't know who brought the news. But it spread like wildfire through the city. People said the ship on which you were journeying from Lanka to Kodikkarai had sunk in the storm at sea. We heard that Periya Pazhuvettaraiyar made every effort to find you, all along the coastline, but even your body could not be recovered. And so, everyone concluded that you had drowned along with the ship. I was on the front steps of this vihara when the news came, and I was beside myself with grief, when one of the monks came running to me and said a boat bearing a very sick man was waiting in the canal by the back of the vihara. I hurried to the spot, only to realise that the sick man was none other than you! It was only after three full days that your fever broke.'

'Acharya! Who brought me here on the boat?'

'Two young people, a man and a woman.'

'Yes, yes, that's what I remember. Do you know who they were? Was the man Vandiyadevan of the Vaanar clan?'

'No, aiya. The man said his name was Senthan Amudan. He seems to be a Shiva devotee. I don't know the woman's identity, but she seemed strong, both of body and mind.'

'I can guess who she was ... the boat-girl Poonguzhali. She is the daughter of Tyagavidangar, who is in charge of the lighthouse in Kodikkarai. Did they not tell you why they brought me here?'

'No, ilavarase. And I didn't ask them either.'

'And you haven't told anyone that I'm here, safe and sound?'

'No, aiya. They had cautioned me not to tell anyone. And given how ill you were, I thought it was most prudent not to tell anyone either.'

'Acharya! There seems to be a conspiracy afoot. My father had sent orders for my arrest. I left Lanka in order to obey him. But all sorts of things occurred on the way. It seems there is a conspiracy to make it appear that I have flouted the emperor's orders. And someone has started a rumour that I have drowned. Gurudeva! Your taking me in will be seen as an act of treachery. And having hidden me here for all these days will only compound the crime. Please send me to Thanjavur right away!'

'Ilavarase! If I am to be punished for having housed you at the vihara, I will consider it an honour. Even if this vihara were to be demolished, it does not matter to me. I ...'

'Gurudeva! I admire and applaud your compassion. Even so, why did you take me in without making any enquiries of the people who brought me here?'

'What need did I have to make enquiries? Bhikshus like me are obliged to cure those who are ill. And what greater honour could we have asked for than taking care of you? Besides, your sister Kundavai Devi had already sent word that you might have to stay here for a few days.'

'Is that so? Was it really Ilaiya Piraatti who sent word? When?'

'Some days before you arrived. Senthan Amudan, for his part, said he was acting in accordance with Ilaiya Piraatti's wishes too.'

'Gurudeva! Did the two people who brought me here leave right away? Can we find them now? I must speak to them and understand what has happened!'

'Aiya, there is no need for panic. The two of them are in town. They come once a day to ask after your health. For some reason, they haven't turned up yet today.'

At this point, the junior monk entered and conveyed something to the Acharya Bhikshu with signs and gestures.

'I'll be back in a bit, aiya,' the Acharya Bhikshu said, and left the room.

When he returned, he saw the prince was even more restless than before.

'Acharya! I cannot stay here a moment longer. I don't wish to be accused of flouting the emperor's orders and hiding here. I don't wish for any ill to come to this ancient vihara on my account.'

The Acharya Bhikshu smiled and said, 'Well, I cannot take on that responsibility any longer either. I do not wish to keep you here against your will. You can leave right away. The boat is waiting for you in the canal.'

'To take me where?'

'That is up to you. The two people who brought you here are in the boat to escort you from here too.'

The prince hesitated. The Acharya Bhikshu's mysterious smile unnerved him. Could there be another conspiracy here, he wondered.

'Both of them came here? Didn't they tell you why they wanted to take me away?'

'They did. There is a Nandi mandapam about a naazhigai's journey down the canal from here. I believe two women are waiting there to see you.'

The prince hurried off the bed. 'Acharya! Please take me to the boat right away. There has already been too long a delay!'

The Acharya Bhikshu led the prince to the canal, holding him by the arm to support him. However, the prince's body bore no indication of having been laid low by a raging fever.

When Senthan Amudan and Poonguzhali saw the prince striding towards them, their faces lit up with joy.

As Arulmozhi Varman sat inside the boat, the Acharya Bhikshu said, 'Aiya! If the monks of the Choodamani Vihara can render you any further service, we would be most honoured. It would be best for you to come back and rest for a week after you have been to the Nandi mandapam.'

'Gurudeva! I have a feeling I will return. If that were not the case, I would not be leaving in such a hurry, without so much as taking my leave of your shishyas,' the prince said.

As the boat left the shore, the prince looked at Poonguzhali and Senthan Amudan in turn and said, 'When you brought me down this canal to the vihara, I thought you had been sent down from Devalokam to escort me to the heavens. But you let me down. You escorted me to a monastery, of all places. Well, that's as may be. The last thing I remember clearly is fighting to stay afloat at sea. I remember my arms flailing as they lost strength. I must know everything that happened since. But, before all that, tell me ... who are these people who are waiting for me at the Nandi mandapam?'

Poonguzhali remained silent.

It was Senthan Amudan who told the prince that Kundavai Piraatti and the Kodumbalur princess had come to Anaimangalam, and were waiting at the Nandi mandapam there.

'Aha! Why has my sister brought along that girl who faints at the slightest provocation?'

'Aiya,' Senthan Amudan said, 'a fever is spreading among the women of Tamizhagam. They want to renounce Shaivism to join the Buddhist order and become bhikshunis.'

'Oh, is that so? Who are these women?'

'I hear that the Kodumbalur princess has expressed such a wish. So has this girl sitting here.'

'That's just two of them, isn't it, Amuda? Well, it's not a loss for Shaivism, anyway. It so happens I know plenty of viharas in Lanka, where bhikshunis lead their ascetic and pious lives. I would be happy to escort these two women there so they can join the order,' Ponniyin Selvan said.

Senthan Amudan laughed.

Then, he proceeded to fill the prince in on everything that had transpired since he and Vandiyadevan had been rescued. The prince listened eagerly, and tried to recall the events as they were narrated.

'There!' Poonguzhali said suddenly. 'That is the Nandi mandapam!'

22

'THE NANDI IS GROWING!'

The bank rose high on either side of the canal. Poonguzhali was pointing at a bathing ghat, with steps leading down from a mandapam. The point at which the steps flattened out onto the mandapam had been decorated with two Nandi statues, one on each side of the steps. One could stare at those statues all day. They were ornate sculptures with a vibrant, lifelike aspect. It was these impressive statues that had given the ghat its name, Nandi mandapam.

Once a year, during the spring festival, the presiding deities of the Tirunagaikaronam[1] temple, Kayarohana Swami and Nilayatakshi Amman, would be brought to the mandapam, where they would remain for several days. People would come in great numbers to see the deities in the mandapam, and then have their dinner under the moonlight before leaving. Since the mandapam was some distance from the city, it didn't see much footfall outside of the festival days.

The boat neared the mandapam.

Once he caught sight of the two women at the ghat, the prince could think of nothing else.

Kundavai Devi began to descend the stairs to receive the boat, even as Vanathi stayed back at the mandapam, half-hidden behind a pillar.

The boat arrived at the steps and stopped. Senthan Amudan helped the prince out of the boat, while his sister held out her hands to help him onto the steps. Having left the prince with Ilaiya Piraatti, Poonguzhali and Senthan Amudan rowed the boat some distance away.

'Thambi! How thin you've become ...' Ilaiya Piraatti said, tears welling up in her eyes and sobs making their way into her voice.

'Well, let's speak about my body later, but what has become of your face? Why do you look so jaded and pale? Your face usually lights up when you see me, but now it is as if clouds have assembled before the moon. And you're in tears! A lot must have happened to have hurt you and worried you in the time I've been away, or you wouldn't have sent me such an urgent message,' Ponniyin Selvan said.

'Yes, thambi, there is much to be said and heard urgently!' his sister replied. 'O epitome of magnanimity, who turned down the golden throne of Lanka, please be seated on this throne of black stone!'

As Ponniyin Selvan laughed and sat down on a step, he touched his sister's feet and raised his hands to his eyes. Kundavai placed his palm on his cheeks and kissed the top of his head. Her eyes were welling up again.

Once she sat down beside him, Kundavai said, 'Thambi! I should never have asked you to come here today. The Acharya Bhikshu of the Choodamani Vihara said you had been cured. But your body has wasted away! I knew you had a terrible fever, but I wasn't able to go without meeting you any longer. Upon arriving in Anaimangalam, every moment felt like a whole yuga to me.'

'Akka! Please don't regret having asked me here. If you hadn't sent the boat, I would have been on my way to Pazhaiyarai by now. Even when I was delirious, the contents of the olai you sent me kept coming back to me and troubling me. And the messenger you sent it with ... that Vandiyadevar[2] of the Vaanar clan ... I've never seen so daring a man as he. I put him to the test in every way I could, and he passed with flying colours every time. Where is he now, Akka?'

The clouds that were shrouding the moon-like face of his sister lifted slightly. She parted her coral lips into a smile and her white teeth shone as she said, 'Thambi! Why worry about him now? There are so many more important things to discuss!'

'Why do you say that, Akka? You seem displeased ... Has he offended you in some way?'

'No, no, not at all! Why should I be displeased? He promised to bring you back with him, and he has fulfilled that promise.'

'And the plots and plans, the mantra and tantra that went into fulfilling that promise astound me even now. Where *is* he, Akka? When I was told you were here, I assumed Vandiyadevar would have accompanied you. Instead, you've brought along the queen of fainting fits!'

'You don't know what a braveheart she has become now, thambi! Yesterday, the prime minister's elephant tossed her into the air. Well, tossed her right into my lap in the howdah, but she did not know that. If only you had seen how boldly she faced that ...'

'Enough, stop praising your friend. I want to hear about *my* friend!'

'What about him? The task he was assigned has been completed. He has returned to his master, Aditya Karikalan.'

'Well, in that case, he has gone back on his word. He said he would not go to Kanchi, and that he would remain in Chozha Naadu.'

'How is that possible? What would he do in Chozha Naadu anyway? No one knows what is going to become of anyone here tomorrow. If you like him so much, why don't you speak to the Chakravarti and give him back the kingdom his ancestors once ruled?'

'And what will that great warrior do with a kingdom, Akka?'

'Whatever all suzerain kings do, that's what! You refused the Lankan throne. You think your friend will do the same with the Vaanar throne, do you?'

The prince smiled and said, 'Akka! I refused the Lankan throne in the presence of witnesses. And yet my father has accused me of conspiracy and sent men to arrest me.'

'Thambi, if you had accepted the throne, he could not have ordered your arrest. You would have been an independent king in your own right. Who could have arrested you then?'

'And you would have me act against our father's wishes?'

'Ponniyin Selva! If you had accepted the Lankan throne, our father would have been happy. He would have then split the Chozha empire between our brother and Madurantakan and been at peace. Efforts are being made in that direction even now. They want to split the empire so that the territories north of the Kollidam river go to one of them, and the territories to the south go to the other. Our father thought you would help him with this. You refused to return when he first sent for you, which is why he ordered your arrest. He is aware that you turned down the Lankan throne.'

'I would never, ever help him split the kingdom into two. There could be no greater crime. It would be preferable to hand over the entire empire to our chithappa, Madurantakan.'

'Then you and the prime minister are on the same page.'

'Yes, the prime minister shares my opinion. He spoke to me about this when he came to Lanka. Akka!

Shall I tell you the true reason for my refusing the Lankan throne?'

'Whom would you tell if not me?'

'True, I have no other confidant. I had heard so much about Lanka before I journeyed there ... it was only when I saw it for myself that I realised how tiny it was. Why, you could ride a horse or elephant from the west coast and reach the east coast of the land in a single day!'

'Well, how much bigger is Chozha Naadu, thambi? Can't one cross the entire expanse of our empire on horseback in a day?'

'True, Chozha Naadu is tiny too. So even if someone were to offer me the Chozha throne, I would refuse. When they split Tamizhagam into three— Chozha Naadu, Pandiya Naadu and Chera Naadu— they committed a terrible crime. That is why, even though this land has birthed fearless warriors and astute rulers, it hasn't made an impression on the rest of the world. Look at the emperors of the north ... Chandragupta, Ashoka, Samudra Gupta, Vikramaditya, Harshavardhan! What grand empires those men forged and ruled! Has any Tamil ruler commanded such a vast empire? The Pallavas of Kanchi produced the likes of Mahendra Chakravarti and Mamallar, who might count ... but then those empires dwindled too. If I am to rule an empire, it won't be such a puny one. It must stretch from Lanka to Ganga, from Malatheevu[3] to Savagatheevu[4]. When the tiger flag flies over every one of those lands, I will ascend the throne … You think I'm a madman, don't you?'

'No, Arulmozhi Varma! I'm happy that there is another person like me, with a penchant for building castles in the air and conjuring up daydreams. If you're a madman, I'm a madwoman, madder than you. I know that our great-grandfather Parantaka Chakravarti nursed such ambitions. He wasn't able to realise them in his lifetime, but I'll witness those dreams come true in *my* lifetime. I will see the Chozha empire stretch from Lanka to Ganga and Malatheevu to Savagam before I die. I once believed Aditya Karikalan would make these dreams come true. But he has no control over his mind, his emotions. And so, he cannot achieve truly great things. I wish to see you realise those dreams. But that might not happen. Even so, I will not be disillusioned. What you cannot achieve, your son will. From the day he is born, I will take responsibility for him, and raise him as he should be raised. I will make him a warrior the like of whom the world has never seen before. I will turn him into a lion who has no time for the little things, and who dreams big, who …'

'Akka! You are certainly madder than I. I have no intention of marrying. And here you are, talking of my son! If one of the friends you coddle has ambitions of marrying me and wearing a bejewelled crown and sitting on the throne, those are never going to be realised. Make sure you pass on the message!' Ponniyin

Selvan said, as his eyes strayed to Vanathi, half-hiding behind one of the pillars in the mandapam. The next moment, he trained his eyes on one of the Nandi statues by the steps.

'Akka! There's something I have to tell you. Although Lanka is a small island, the ancient rulers of that empire were grand men. They had big hearts and great dreams. They achieved some amazing feats. They built stupas of red brick that reach into the skies. They built Buddhist viharas with thousands of rooms. They built mandapams with ten thousand pillars. As if to show just how great a god, how great a man, Buddha was. I have seen Buddha statues taller than coconut trees, Akka! You see this Nandi statue? Look how small it is. And this is supposed to be the vahana of Mahadeva, whose head and feet Vishnu and Brahma failed to find! And Paramashiva's entourage in Kailash comprises Bhoota ganas[5]. Nandi is charged with guarding Shiva's private quarters so that these Bhoota ganas don't bother him. How can such a little Nandi stop the Bhoota ganas from entering? Now, look, Akka! The Nandi is growing right before my eyes. It is becoming huge. It has a gigantic form now, and is hitting the roof of the mandapam. The roof is broken now. Why, Nandi bhagavan has touched the skies. The Bhoota ganas are coming here now. Ah, they are awestruck by the size of Nandi. They bow in deference to him and seek permission to meet Shiva bhagavan. Now, if the lord's vahana is this large, touching the skies, think how large the temple must be to accommodate such a lord! We must build a temple that disappears into the skies, so that it is known as Dakshina Meru! The temples we have in Chozha Naadu right now will barely accommodate Agastya Muni[6]! How will poor Shiva Peruman enter? I don't want the throne or the crown. Whoever sits on the throne and wears the crown should make me the official in charge of Shiva temples, that's all I ask!'

'Thambi, we seem to be competing for the title of maddest in the family! The empire is in great danger at the moment. There are enemies within and enemies without. We are surrounded by peril, in the form of enemies posing as friends. For some time now, I have been having a recurring nightmare. An enormous sword that flashes like lightning appears suddenly before my eyes. It is about to fall on someone. I can't see whom. I don't know whether that is the sword that will claim the life of someone from the Chozha dynasty, or the sword that will split this empire in two and bring it to ruin. It is up to you and me to join forces and prevent such a threat from subsuming Chozha Naadu!'

'Yes, Akka, I had the same sense, of being surrounded by danger, after listening to all that Vandiyadevar had to say. And you're aware of who poses the greatest danger, aren't you?'

'You're referring to Pazhuvoor Ilaiya Rani Nandini, aren't you, thambi?'

'Yes, Akka. And you know who she is, don't you?'

'I learnt the truth from Vandiyadevar. And that is why I was in such a tearing hurry to come see you.'

23

VANATHI IN DANGER

'Akka! Do you remember, I fell into the Kaveri when I was five years old? And Kaveri Amman saved my life and brought me back safely to the boat and then disappeared, do you remember?' Arulmozhi Varman asked.

'What a question, thambi! How could I ever forget? It is because of this incident that we call you "Ponniyin Selvan", isn't it?' Kundavai said.

'I met Kaveri Amman in Lanka,' Arulmozhi Varman said. He waited for his sister's reaction, and then said, 'Why are you silent? Aren't you surprised?'

'No, I'm not. But I'm curious. Tell me everything about her!'

'One day, one conversation, will not allow me to do her justice. I'll give you the gist, though. It wasn't just the one time that she saved my life. She protected me from various dangers and foiled several attempts on my life in Lanka! But it's not simply that, Akka ... it often happens that one saves another's life by chance. It's the affection she has for me, the deep intense love … not in all the fourteen worlds, seven above and seven below, can one find such love … why, I would say …. I would say she loves me even more than you do!'

'Well, you needn't hesitate to say it. My love for you is not so great or pure. It is not without selfishness. I'll tell you the truth, thambi. My first love is for my empire. The Chozha empire's well-being is my first concern. My love for you stems from the fact that you are crucial to the empire. And if it so happens that you turn into an obstacle, my love for you might well transform into hate. But that deaf-mute lady's love is not so. She has transferred all the love she has nursed for our father for the past twenty years, to you. It *is* true that you will not find such love in all fourteen worlds.'

'How do you know this, Akka?'

'Know what, thambi?'

'That she is our Periya Thaayaar[1]?'

'I figured it out from what our father said, and from all that I learned later from Vandiyadevar. Does she think you're her own son? Or that you're the son of the woman who supplanted her as our father's wife?'

'The two have never struck me as different. And I don't think it matters a bit to her. Why do you ask such a question?'

'Thambi, our mother sits on the throne that this lady should have rightfully occupied. Isn't it a wonder that she loves you so much in spite of this?'

'She must know that I am not the son she birthed. How could she not realise that I am not as old as her own son should be? She cannot speak, and so she cannot tell me what is on her mind. I've tried to put two and two together from the paintings she has made and shown me. Leave aside the love she has for me. When I think of how much she must care for our father, my heart melts. Akka, when Appa was my age, did he look like I do?'

'No, thambi, no! When Appa was your age, he was so handsome that even Manmadha could not compete with him for beauty. Our Chozha dynasty is famous for courage, but not for good looks. Our grandfather Arinjayar married the pulchritudinous Kalyani of the Vaidumba clan, unrivalled in beauty. They say her skin was as smooth as pure gold, her face as lovely as the full moon. Even now, at her age, Kalyani Patti is so beautiful! Can you imagine how she must have looked in her youth? Our father inherited her looks, and became known as "Sundara Chozhar". The three of us take after our mother. The progeny of Tirukkovalur Malayalaman are disgusted by beauty; they believe it is the opposite of bravery.'

'I don't know whether beauty and bravery have anything to do with each other, but I do know that appearance and affection are unrelated. If that were not the case ...'

'If that were not the case, why should Vanathi stare at you without even blinking, hidden behind the pillar? And why should Senthan Amudan not to be able to tear his eyes away from that girl Poonguzhali, sitting in the boat?'

The prince smiled and said, 'Akka! Look where you've taken this conversation! I was talking about my Periya Thaayaar's affection for me. Well, anyway … do you think two people can look exactly alike?'

'Why not? If they're twins, it's possible. And it is also possible for mother and daughter to look exactly alike. And then, there are times when people who are unrelated to each other look like twins too.'

'Could it be true that our Periya Thaayaar looks exactly like Pazhuvoor Ilaiya Rani, as Vandiyadevar claims? I haven't seen Nandini since she was a young girl. I haven't got a good look at her since she became the Pazhuvoor Ilaiya Rani. What is your opinion?'

'Well, I've seen the Pazhuvoor Ilaiya Rani, but not our Periya Thaayaar. But Vandiyadevar must be right. From what our father told me, it makes sense.'

'Our father told you? What did he tell you? And when?'

'A while ago, Vanathi and I had gone to Thanjavur. He spoke of an incident that had occurred in his youth. He told me of how he had once been stranded on an island off the main coast of Lanka, and how a deaf-mute woman had looked after him there. And then, how Parantaka Chakravarti's men had arrived and found him there, and taken him back to Chozha Naadu. On the day he was made the crown prince, he caught sight of her among the people who thronged the streets to watch the coronation. But she disappeared right away. He sent Aniruddhar to search her out and bring her back. But Aniruddhar came back with the news that the lady had jumped off the lighthouse into the sea, and drowned to her death. Our father has been haunted by this tragedy and his guilt for twenty-four years. Our father believes she is dead, and that he was the cause of her suicide. Thambi, before we speak of our dreams of expansion for the Chozha empire, we have an important filial duty to carry out. You must bring that lady, that queen among women, somehow or the other, from Lanka. We must prove to our father that she is still alive. Or, our father will not know peace in this life or the next!'

'Akka, I have been at death's door a few times in the last weeks. Do you know the foremost thought in my mind through all that time? That I would die without having reunited Periamma with Appa. Akka! My heart aches for that lovely woman. If only she could speak, she could seek solace by telling us of the worries and hurt and grief and sorrow she nurses all by herself. Think of the predicament of someone who is deaf-mute. The love and enthusiasm and sorrow and hurt and anger and pangs of yearning they feel must be dammed up within their hearts. And in the case of our Periamma, who has suffered such a terrible betrayal ... can you imagine what she must feel? Is it any surprise that she roams the forests of Lanka like a madwoman? When I think about all this, I feel as if my heart will actually burst from sorrow. I want to bring her to our father, to reunite them, somehow or the other. But do you think this is what our father wants, Akka?'

'Whether he wants it or not, it is our duty. Our father screams and sobs at night, believing her ghost is haunting him. And it is because of this that his health refuses to improve.'

'How do you know this, Akka? Did our father tell you this too?'

'He did, and so did my friend Vanathi.'

'Vanathi told you? But what does she have to do with any of this? Did you tell her everything?'

'No, no! We were staying at the Thanjavur palace … wait, I'll get her to recount the events for you herself. Thambi! I must say I'm shocked by your behaviour. You seem to have forgotten the forms and manners for which our Chozha clan is known. You haven't spoken a word to the Kodumbalur princess in all this time. Not so much as a "How do you do?" Is this all the respect you have for the daughter of the great martyr, Kodumbalur Siriya Velaar?'

'Akka, when you're there to look after Vanathi, what is the point of my asking how she is? What could she possibly lack?'

'Excellent question! Now you stay quiet. Vanathi! Come here! The prince wishes to get a good look at you!' Kundavai called to her.

Vanathi came closer. She said, neither able to look at the prince nor look away, 'Akka! You're imagining things. Your brother does not wish to see me. He only has eyes for the boat in the canal. He seems to be in a hurry to return.'

When she spoke of the boat, was she speaking of the boat-girl Poonguzhali, who was seated inside?

The prince said with a laugh, 'Akka! It appears your friend can speak. I'd been wondering if she was another one of the deaf-mute ladies we've been coming across of late.'

'Akka! Every time I see him, I lose my powers of speech,' Vanathi said. 'Sometimes, I myself wonder whether I'm mute after all.'

'That's very good. There is a man in Kodikkarai … Poonguzhali's brother, in fact. He manages to speak to everyone else. But the moment his wife makes an appearance, he loses his power of speech. So, everyone in his family has concluded that he is mute.'

'This Kodumbalur girl is somewhat like that. Earlier, she would chatter non-stop. She couldn't keep quiet even if asked to stay silent for a bit. And once she started yapping, she just couldn't stop. But ever since you first left for Lanka, she has been speaking less and less. She wanders off by herself, immersed in thought. Well, let's leave all that aside for now. Vanathi, tell the prince exactly what you saw that night, at the Thanjavur palace.'

'Akka, let the princess take a seat and then tell the story. If her uncle were to see her remain standing all this while, he would crumble from sorrow. Every time the senapati sees me, he asks after her. But you never send news of her. And so, I have no answer for him,' the prince said.

'I told the Vaanar hero in great detail about her health. Did he not tell you?'

'He must have, Akka. But the prince would not have paid attention. He has other worries,' Vanathi said.

'That is true. Once I read your olai, I couldn't think of anything else. And the fever seems to have left me rather hard of hearing. Ask your friend to speak up, will you?' Arulmozhi Varman said.

Vanathi went on to recount all that she had seen on the day Kundavai had gone to the Durga temple ... how she had heard the emperor wail in his room, how she had gone to take a look and what she had seen there. Every time Vanathi happened to look at the prince's face during this narration, she would be so transfixed she would trail off. Ilaiya Piraatti had to bring her back to Earth and urge her to continue.

The prince listened keenly, and then said, 'Akka! Your friend seems to have left out something important. Surely, once she had heard and seen all that she did, she must have collapsed in a faint?'

Kundavai laughed. Vanathi was so embarrassed she kept her eyes trained on the ground.

Ilaiya Piraatti then turned to her and said in a voice brimming with affection, 'Vanathi! Why don't you go for a short walk by the shore? Or, if you'd rather, go join our entourage. The prince will remain here for some days. You can meet again.'

'Akka, I'll go for a walk,' Vanathi said, and skipped away.

What had filled her with so much cheer that there was joy in every step she took? Arulmozhi Varman watched her leave, her face glowing and eyes wide. Once she had disappeared, he turned to his sister.

'Akka,' he said, 'I see why our father was upset. But what do you think he saw? Whose form did he see? Was it a hallucination? In that case, how could your friend have seen it too?'

'It was not a hallucination, neither for our father nor for Vanathi. It was a drama staged at midnight for the emperor. And the leading lady was the Pazhuvoor Ilaiya Rani Nandini. I had guessed it back then. But after hearing what you and Vandiyadevar have to say, I am absolutely certain of it.'

'Why would they stage such a drama? Why should the Pazhuvoor Rani put on such a show?'

'Nandini has some suspicions about her birth. Chakravarti had once lost consciousness upon seeing her. She has avoided appearing before him since. She probably planned this in the hope that his reaction might reveal some truth.'

'Do you think it worked, Akka?'

'I don't know. What goes on in her mind and heart is a mystery even to the creator, Brahma. When I think of Pazhuvettaraiyar's predicament, I feel sorry for him. Thambi, we were speaking of beauty some time ago, weren't we? Nandini has a monopoly on beauty among women. The rest of us are as dust at her feet. Every man who sees her promptly becomes her slave. Pazhuvettaraiyar, Madurantakar, Tirumalaiyappan, Kandan Maaran and now Parthibendran! The prime minister is so scared of her charisma that he doesn't dare go anywhere near her. And for the same reason, Aditya Karikalan does not come to Thanjavur. Thambi, there is only one man who is not scared of Nandini's beauty, who has not been tricked by her, who has escaped her clutches …'

'Our Vaanar hero, you mean?'

'Exactly. That is why I have sent him to Aditya Karikalan in Kanchi.'

'What for?'

'The Pazhuvoor Rani has invited our brother to Kadambur Sambuvarayar's palace. I have sent Vandiyadevar to prevent the two of them from meeting. And even if they were to meet, to prevent something disastrous from happening. Aditya Karikalan does not know that Nandini is our sister. And I don't know whether she is aware either.'

'Are you certain that she is our sister, Akka?'

'What room is there for doubt? Thambi! Ever since I learned this truth, I have had a complete change of heart. When we were children, I hated Nandini, and humiliated her every chance I got. I was envious of her beauty. I conspired to separate you and Karikalan from her. Even after she went off to Pandiya Naadu, my envy and hatred did not abate. When she married the old man and returned, I mocked and humiliated her. I have decided to make up for it all.'

'How, Akka? How will you make up for it?'

'The next time I meet her, I will fall at her feet and beg her forgiveness for all my wrongdoing. And whatever punishment she gives me, I will accept.'

'And I will stop you. You are guilty of no wrongdoing, and you have no need of begging for anyone's forgiveness. And there is no one in all these fourteen worlds who is fit to punish you. You did not envy Pazhuvoor Ilaiya Rani. It was she who was jealous of you, who hated you.'

'Thambi! You spoke of how your heart breaks for our Periamma, wandering the islands off the Lankan coast like a madwoman. Spare a thought, then, for Nandini. She should have grown up in a palace, with all the luxuries of a royal life … instead, what trials and tribulations she has encountered! My heart feels like it will break when I think about this. The person paying for the error someone else committed long ago is our sister, married to this old man …'

'Akka! Do you have any idea how any of this happened? Why does our father think Periamma is dead? Why did Nandini grow up in someone else's house like an orphan? What brought about such a situation?'

'I wonder about this day and night. But I haven't been able to find out. There are two people in our circle who know something about this. Our Periya Patti Sembiyan Mahadevi is one. She knows some part of all this at least. And the other is the prime minister. I have a feeling Aniruddha Brahmarayar knows the whole story. But there's little chance of us learning the truth from either of them. Azhvarkadiyaan must know something too. He's a vault, though, even more steadfast than his guru. Thambi! There's no hurry for us to learn all this. The priority now is to avert the danger that Nandini poses to our clan. Vandiyadevar told me that she has a sword that glints like lightning, with a fish emblem on it, that she practically worships this sword … I have been in a state ever since I heard of this. What if the Pazhuvoor Rani does something terrible, without knowing that this is the clan of her birth?'

'What if we tell her the whole story?'

'I don't know if that will serve any purpose. Her rage against us might even grow manifold. But we must do our duty nevertheless.'

'You did the right thing in sending Vandiyadevar to our brother. But shouldn't we tell our father too? It's bad enough that he is physically in such bad shape. Why must the mental torment drag on? Shouldn't we leave for Thanjai right away?'

'No, never, thambi! I'm leaving for Thanjai in a couple of days. But you must remain in Choodamani Vihara for a while yet.'

'Why do you say that? You want me to continue flouting our father's orders and to run and hide instead?'

'Yes! If you come to Thanjai now, the entire land will erupt in confusion. Right now, the subjects of Chozha Naadu are furious with the Pazhuvettaraiyars and Madurantakar. They are even angry with our father, for ordering your arrest. If they see you alive, their emotions will run so high that we cannot predict the consequences. What if they demand that you be made the Crown Prince? What if they lay siege to the Thanjavur fort and palace? Our father is already miserable. Can he bear much more hurt? Thambi, I sent a scroll asking you to hurry back because the empire was in great danger. And for that same reason, I feel it would be best for you to return to Lanka.'

'Akka, that is impossible. I will not go back to Lanka without meeting our father. If you think it would best for me to go to Thanjavur in secret, I will. But I simply must meet the Chakravarti! I must tell him who Kaveri Amman, the woman who has been keeping me alive all these years, is!'

'I'll find the right time to tell him myself. Why do you insist on going in person?'

'Because that's the only way he will believe it. And that's the only way my mind will be at peace. I can ask his permission to bring Periamma there.'

'Arulvarma! I'm not standing in the way of your wishes. But you must stay at the Choodamani Vihara for another week. I will precede you to Thanjai. I will let our father know that you are here and waiting to meet him. Thambi! I came here not just to see you but also to make a request of you. If you will grant me this one thing, I will never trouble you again. I know it is the lot of men to put themselves in the way of danger. I do want for you to be hailed as a braveheart on the battlefield, a conqueror who epitomises courage. But before you go in search of peril again, please fulfil this one wish of mine.'

'Why are you so afraid I won't fulfil it, Akka? Have I ever refused to honour your wishes?'

'No, and it is from the faith that you will honour this too that I ask you now ... Aditya Karikalan has not married yet. And one doesn't get the impression that he ever will. It is you who must carry on the dynasty, to birth Sundara Chozhar's descendants. You must fulfil my wishes in this matter.'

'And if I consent to this, you will consent to my marrying the woman of my choice, won't you?'

'What a question! For twenty years, you and I have not differed in our views on anything. Why do you ask if I will consent?'

'Akka, there is a specific reason I ask. The girl I marry must share my dreams, don't you think? She must support me, and help me realise them, isn't it?'

'Thambi! Is it with a woman's support that you intend to realise your dreams?'

At that moment, a panicked cry rose. 'Aiyo! Aiyo! Akka! Akka!'

It was Vanathi's voice.

The story continues in
BOOK 7
BEJEWELLED CROWN

An Extract

THE FLYING ARROW

Poonguzhali looked at the Oomai Rani, half-hidden behind a tree on the shore. Encountering her like this, at an unexpected place and hour, startled Poonguzhali for a moment. She knew that her aunt did not like meeting strangers. Senthan Amudan was on the boat. Would her Aththai run away when she saw that Poonguzhali was not alone?

She had barely completed the thought before her aunt took off at a run. Poonguzhali jumped onto the shore and ran to an elevated spot. She saw her aunt disappearing into the forest some distance away.

Senthan Amudan had joined her by now.

'Poonguzhali! Poonguzhali! Who was that, standing here a moment ago?' he asked.

'Couldn't you tell, Amuda?'

'Not for sure. But, perhaps …'

'Yes, my Aththai! And your Periyamma, whom you thought was dead all this while!'

'Yes, I thought I could spot a resemblance to Amma.'

'Oh, please, you're just saying that. Chinna Aththai and Periya Aththai look nothing like each other. There is no similarity in their natures either. That's like comparing a cow tethered in one's backyard to a lioness roaming free!'

'Right, that's as may be. But why did the lioness take off at a run upon seeing you?'

Poonguzhali laughed and said, 'She ran upon seeing *you*! She doesn't like meeting strangers.'

'But I'm not a stranger, am I?'

'How would Aththai know who you are? Until she realises, she will hesitate to come anywhere close. Once I tell her you're her nephew, she won't run away.'

'Poonguzhali, what will you do now?'

'I'm going to go find Aththai.'

'Shall I come along?'

'Why?'

'To meet Periyamma in person.'

'Why should you meet Periyamma?'

Senthan Amudan had been keen to meet his Periyamma after learning something of her past from Poonguzhali. He also hoped she might help him convince Poonguzhali to marry him.

'For several reasons. But does one need a reason to want to meet his own aunt?' he asked.

Poonguzhali thought for a while and then said, 'All right, come along. It will be much harder to catch her if you're with me, but you won't stop badgering me, so let's not waste any more time. We'll secure the boat here and go.'

They hid the boat behind a thazhampoo shrub and made for the Kodikkarai forest.

'You said Periyamma would be either in Bhoota Theevu or the Lankan mainland, didn't you?'

'Yes, she divides her time between the two.'

'Does she come here often?'

'No, very rarely. She comes to check on me if I haven't been to meet her for a long time.'

'And has she come to see you now?'

'I have a feeling she's here for some other reason.'

'What could that be?'

'Perhaps to see whether her beloved adopted son has drowned in the sea or reached the shore safely. Aththai knows there was a tempest after the prince boarded the ship, no?'

'If Arulmozhi Varmar is her adopted son, who is her actual son?'

'I don't know. But I will find out sooner or later.'

'Is her actual son even alive?'

'True, he might be dead, who knows?' Poonguzhali said.

After a while, she said, 'Amuda! You saw Aththai and said she bore some resemblance to your mother. Does someone else's face come to mind?'

'I have a vague feeling that she does remind me of someone else. But I can't tell for sure. It is as if it were hidden behind clouds.'

'Have you seen Pazhuvoor Ilaiya Rani often?'

'I've seen her now and then, yes. Oh! It didn't occur to me until you just mentioned it, but Periyamma *does* look like Nandini Devi! How strange! How is that possible, Poonguzhali? And how did you notice the resemblance?'

'I meet Aththai often. And I saw the Pazhuvoor Ilaiya Rani only some days ago, right here in Kodikkarai. Their facial resemblance struck me right away.'

'What could the reason be?'

'That's another thing I'll find out sooner or later. I'm planning to ask Aththai about it when I meet her today.'

'But Aththai is mute. How will she respond?'

'Don't you speak to your mother?'

'Yes. Through signs and gestures. But I've been doing it all my life. Even so, I struggle when I have to convey something out of the ordinary.'

'Periya Aththai and I talk through signs and gestures too. And what we can't convey through those, we tell through paintings.'

'What an awful thing for both sisters to be deaf-mute! How much sorrow it must have brought their parents!'

'And that's not all. All through their childhood, the two sisters fought all the time. That's why our grandfather went away with Periya Aththai and settled in Bhoota Theevu. He was particularly fond of her. Some astrologer had told him when she was an infant that she was born to be queen. When he found out she was mute, he was devastated.'

They entered the forest as they spoke, and began their search for the Oomai Rani. But the hours passed, and yet there was no sign of Oomai Rani.

'Amuda! We aren't able to find Aththai because of your presence. She must have hidden herself somewhere after seeing you.'

'Just my luck. Nothing I want materialises. All right, shall I leave then?'

'How will you find your way out? It is I who must guide you.'

At that very moment, a strange cry rose from inside the forest. It sounded neither human nor bestial. The cry was repeated a couple of times. A herd of deer went flying in the direction from which the voice came.

Poonguzhali thought for some time, and then said, 'Amuda! Follow me silently.'

The two of them walked as quietly as they could in the direction from which the cry had come. It was not long before they came upon a bizarre sight.

The Oomai Rani was leaning against a tree, holding out some grass. The deer stood all around her, eating from her hands. On her shoulders, she straddled a little fawn, who was staring at her face with beautiful, large eyes.

Poonguzhali and Amudan stood in silence, gazing upon this incredible sight. It was the fawn that first spotted them, and jumped off Oomai Rani's shoulders and onto the ground right away. This drew the attention of the other deer to the intruders. The animals stood poised to run if they approached. Finally, the Oomai Rani saw them too, and let out another strange sound from her throat. At this, the entire herd of deer fled.

'The only language Aththai doesn't speak is that of humans. She can communicate with every other species in their languages,' Poonguzhali said, and began to communicate with her aunt through gestures of the hand.

This time, her aunt did not run. She responded to Poonguzhali with gestures of her own.

Then, Poonguzhali went up to her. Her aunt embraced her and kissed the top of her head. Senthan Amudan remained waiting some distance away.

The two women spoke in sign language for some time, and then Poonguzhali beckoned to Amudan, asking him to join them.

At first, the Oomai Rani looked him up and down a few times, and then placed her palm on his head as if to bless him. She then took her hand away and grabbed Poonguzhali, urgently leading her somewhere. Senthan followed them.

The three of them reached the shore. The Oomai Rani sat down and conveyed something to Poonguzhali, who then said, 'Amuda, come, let's go home. Aththai refuses to come with us. She wants us to bring her some food instead.'

The two of them made for the lighthouse.

'Poonguzhali, what are your plans now?' Amudan asked.

'I did want to come to Thanjai with you. But now, I can't. Aththai wants to meet her beloved adopted son. So, I'll have to go back to Nagapattinam. It's best you don't come along. I have a lot of questions for Aththai, and she'll only answer me in private.'

Senthan Amudan heaved a sigh and said, 'Just my luck. All right, then, I'll say goodbye right away.'

'No, no! Come home, have some food and take your leave of everyone at home. Otherwise, they'll start fighting with me.'

On their way to the lighthouse, they came across another strange sight. In the shadow of a bush, partially hidden from sight, stood a man and woman, talking.

Aha! It seems to be Anni Rakkammaal, Poonguzhali thought. *So, her secret meetings continue. Who is that with her? A spy from Pandiya Naadu? Or someone else?*

Rakkammaal parted the bush and stepped out. Her eyes fell on Poonguzhali, and she seemed startled. But she recovered quickly, and approached the two of them.

'Poonguzhali! Where were you all this while? Your father and brother have been so anxious!' she said.

'Why? Is this the first time I've left home?'

'This time, you took your Aththai's son along, no? They were worried that you've eloped and married him!'

'Anni! How many times have I told you not to talk this sort of rubbish! If you do this again ...'

'No, penne, I won't! What do I care if you marry your Aththai's son? Or a prince, for that matter? Your Periya Aththai came in search of you from Lanka. Did you meet her?'

'No, not yet,' Poonguzhali said.

The moment she got a chance to speak to Amudan alone, she whispered, 'Amuda! Careful! Anni is in cahoots with those spies from Pandiya Naadu. She'll try to draw you out and get information from you about what we've been up to. Don't answer her!'

'I might as well join the mutes in our family, for whatever time I'm here,' Amudan said.

~*~

That afternoon, Poonguzhali left for Nagapattinam with her aunt. Typically, she would feel calm and relaxed in the Oomai Rani's company. The two of them had a rapport, and it was as if their hearts were in sync. But this time, that sense of peace eluded her.

She often thought about how she had rowed Ponniyin Selvan along the same route, when he had been burning with fever. When it struck her that she had gone to all that trouble, only for him to choose a princess over her, she felt a stab of pain in her chest.

The manner in which she had practically pushed Senthan Amudan away, insisting he go back home, also made her feel guilty.

There was another thought that troubled her. It was what her father had said as she was leaving.

Uncharacteristically, he had warned her against setting off alone. 'My child!' he had said. 'It would be a good idea not to go back and forth so much. All sorts of strangers have been frequenting this place. No one seems to know why they're here or at whose instance. People speak of conspiracy in the palace corridors. Please don't get drawn into such things. Our family is obligated to serve the Chozha clan. We are forever indebted to them for many, many things. Don't forget that!'

Her sister-in-law's secret rendezvous made Poonguzhali uneasy. Perhaps those strangers had been looking for Poonguzhali, in the hope that she would lead them to Prince Arulmozhi Varmar? How terrible it would be if she was the one who gave him away!

As if all this were not enough, she could hear rustling sounds coming from the banks. There was no breeze at all. It was as if the wind was being held ransom. What was causing the rustling in the undergrowth, then? The Oomai Rani was, naturally, untroubled by all this for she couldn't hear anything. There was no point in asking her what she made of it.

Yet, her aunt had some superpowers. Her eyesight was so sharp it all but made up for her deafness. And she seemed to have a sixth sense. Surely, as long as the Oomai Rani was around, nothing could happen to either of them?

But then ... her Aththai was also looking towards the shore, with a worried expression. Were they being pursued, then?

Soon, though, she realised why her aunt had been looking at the shore. And it came as a relief.

A group of five or six deer stood among the bushes along the bank, peering at the boat. No, they were not peering at the boat, but at the Oomai Rani! Aha ... what beautiful creatures deer were! Why had the same God who had created these lovely animals also chosen to create such an ugly species as the human? Unworthy beings! Why, there were people who actually hunted deer! How could one bring oneself to kill these innocent, beautiful animals?

As she marvelled at the deer, Poonguzhali was so lost in her thoughts that she stopped rowing.

The boat came to a halt.

All of a sudden, a guttural scream emerged from the Oomai Rani's throat, different from what Poonguzhali and Amudan had heard in the morning. There was panic and urgency in that cry, as if she was trying to warn someone. The deer sensed her panic and began to run.

At that moment, they heard the whizz of an arrow being shot. The arrow flew and hit one of the deer, which let out a moan. The Oomai Rani leapt from the boat onto the shore and made for the wounded deer.

As she was nearing the animal, there was a mad rustling in the bushes. Seven or eight men suddenly surrounded her. Many of them held spears. Not far off stood Rakkammaal, who must have guided them to the spot.

The Oomai Rani tried to escape, but couldn't move. When she realised it was pointless, she stood still. Two men stepped forward and bound her arms with rope.

All this occurred within seconds.

As soon as Poonguzhali saw them tying her aunt up, she leapt onto the shore herself, oar in hand to serve as a weapon.

Five men broke away from the group and ran towards Poonguzhali. They caught her and carried her to the boat, where they bound her tightly with rope. Then, they left, along with the Oomai Rani.

NOTES

1. VANATHI

1. The wife of Satyavan, who famously tricked Yama into giving her husband his life back; however, one may assume the husband's temporary death caused her a fair bit of grief.

2. The wife of Raja Harishchandra—the king's proclivity for telling the truth caused his wife and child a fair bit of pain.

3. The 'other woman' in *Silappadikaram*, a courtesan who became Kovalan's lover.

4. Kovalan's long-suffering wife from *Silappadikaram*, who first lost her husband to Madhavi and later to death.

5. Vadivelar and Kartikeya are both names given to the mythological god Muruga, whose two wives are Valli and Deivanai. Valli had fallen in love with him when they had both been celestial beings, but a curse had required that they only be united in a mortal birth. Valli was born (in a hunter's family), apparently with the knowledge that she would have to wait a couple of dozen years to marry the love of her life—not a situation one would envy. Deivanai had it easier; she was Valli's sister by birth, but was adopted by Indra,

who didn't have much trouble arranging an alliance for her with Muruga.

6. Readers might remember that the titular name of Boothi Vikrama Kesari is 'Kodumbalur Periya Velaar'. Vanathi's father was his younger brother.

7. This is a traditional poetic comparison, that of a woman's midriff to a leaf known as the 'aalilai'. The aalilai is the leaf of the banyan tree, the shape of which is said to be the most desired for that part of a woman's body, between the breasts and hip. Presumably, these are virgin women, or at least women who have not yet given birth, because no woman who has birthed a child can hope to have that shape of stomach without a little help from her surgeons.

2. VANATHI REGAINS CONSCIOUSNESS

1. The mythological six-tusked elephant that is believed to be the mount of Indra, king of the devas.

4. ANIRUDDHAR'S PLEA

1. It is of note that the prime minister uses the familiar singular to address Kundavai Devi, although she is the princess. It speaks to his closeness to her father, and his status in the royal household and, therefore, in the empire.

2. The Ionians, the earliest known Greeks to have attempted conquest of these parts.

3. The Hephthalites.

5. KUNDAVAI IN TORMENT

1. A corruption of 'Harishchandra'—the river was named after the king who insisted on speaking the truth and

nothing but the truth, usually—and predictably—to his detriment.

8. TWO PRISONS

1. One of the types of Tamil folk songs. It is considered to be derived either from 'theyn paangu'—as sweet as honey—or 'then paangu'—of the southern region. It is a type of breezy song, which people sing to relieve themselves of stress as they work in the fields, or go on long journeys. It may be sung by a single person, or in the form of a proposition and response or question and answer, between two or more people.

2. There is a slightly different explanation for this song in Chapter 6 of Book 4, *Wind Storm*, an interpretation of its meaning and context given by Azhvarkadiyaan.

3. Literally, 'Does a lock exist that can contain love?'

4. This is a folktale associated with the deity of Shiva at the Meenakshi Amman temple in Madurai. A Pandiya king apparently wanted to see a large procession of horses and was willing to pay a hefty sum for it. For reasons unknown, Shiva took on the form of a horse trader and sold the king a number of magnificent horses, only for them to turn into foxes on the day of the procession. Then, Shiva apparently revealed his true form and then turned the foxes back into horses. The king was poorer by whatever sum he had given the 'horse trader', and perhaps left confused about the lesson he was to learn from the episode, as most of us are.

5. The word 'thai' means 'mother'. This is the first time Kundavai has spoken of her with such respect.

9. A LADY IN GREEN SILK

1. The seventh month in the Tamil calendar, corresponding roughly to the period from mid-October to mid-November.

11. VANATHI ASKS A FAVOUR

1. The daughter born to Kovalan and Madhavi from *Silappadhikaram*, and the protagonist of its sequel *Manimeghalai*, written by Seeththalai Saathanaar.

2. Although the word 'espionage' could have been used here, the Tamil word 'otraadal' appears as an innovation to Vandiyadevan, and that literally translates into 'spyology'. I have retained it for both comic effect, and to create a more authentic effect of surprise and a sense of how bizarre such a concept must sound to Vandiyadevan.

3. *Tirukkural* has been attributed to the poet Valluvar, often referred to as 'Tiruvalluvar'. Tiruvalluvar, however, is also known by several other names, including Poyyamozhi Pulavar, Deiva Pulavar, Poyyil Pulavar, Perunavalar, Devar, Nayanar and Sennabodhar. *Tirukkural* itself comprises 1,330 couplets of seven words each, four in the first line and three in the second, each line containing approximately the same number of syllables, although of different lengths in appearance.

13. 'THE TIME IS NIGHT!'

1. This term of endearment refers to the pupil of the eye; it is a term of enormous affection, and I chose to retain it over 'darling' or 'dear'.
2. The equivalent of Saturday in Tamil.

14. A FIGURE IN THE DARK

1. This word can mean many things, ranging from 'young' to 'son', by way of 'prince'. In this context, it may be roughly translated as, 'My son'.

15. A DISGUISE EXPOSED

1. This word used to be inaccurately translated as 'genuflections', but now it has been made famous in the West as 'super brain yoga'. It is usually either done as a sign of repentance in temples, particularly Vinayaka temples, or imposed as punishment by a child's parents or teachers.

17. GAJENDRA MOKSHAM

1. The andril bird is an important symbol of love in Tamil poetry of the Sangam era. I retained the original Tamil words instead of using 'the glossy ibis' because of this reference. Andril birds mate for life. It is said that if a bird's mate were to die, the bird would die right away too.

19. MADURANTAKAN'S GRATITUDE

1. This was meant as a compliment, not necessarily backhanded. 'Rajatantram' is synonymous with 'Chanakya tantram' or 'Chanakya tantra', where deception and lies and pragmatism were prioritised in the management of the royal court.
2. This is one of the 1,331 couplets known as the *Tirukkural*.
3. New moon.

22. 'THE NANDI IS GROWING!'

1. Another term for Nagapattinam.
2. Although the prince is of a much higher rank than a soldier, it is notable that he speaks of Vandiyadevan in the respectful form, using the '-r' ending, rather than '-n'—the equivalent of the English 'mister' or 'esquire' and the equivalent of the Hindi '-ji' suffix.
3. Modern-day Maldives.
4. Modern-day Indonesia.
5. The Bhoota ganas are one of the eighteen 'ganas', in the classification of celestials. These include the devas, asuras, nagas and various others.
6. Agastya is the shortest of the seven sages, or the Saptarishi.

23. VANATHI IN DANGER

1. 'Thaayaar' is a deferential word for 'mother'. 'Periya' means big, and can refer to the elder sister of one's mother, the wife of one's father's older brother or, as in this case, the senior wife of one's father.

Also from ekadā

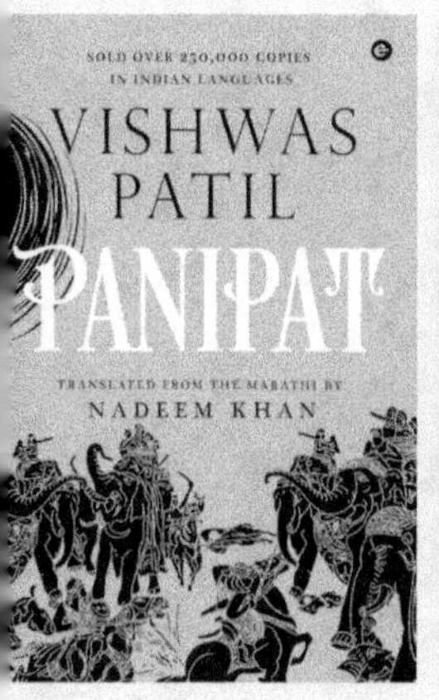

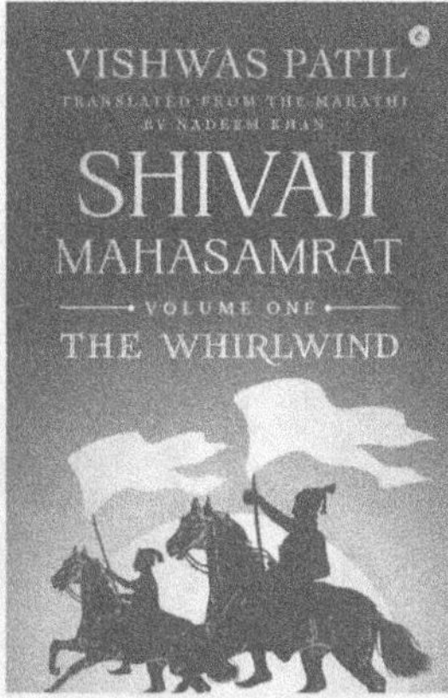

Also from ekadā

Also from ekadā

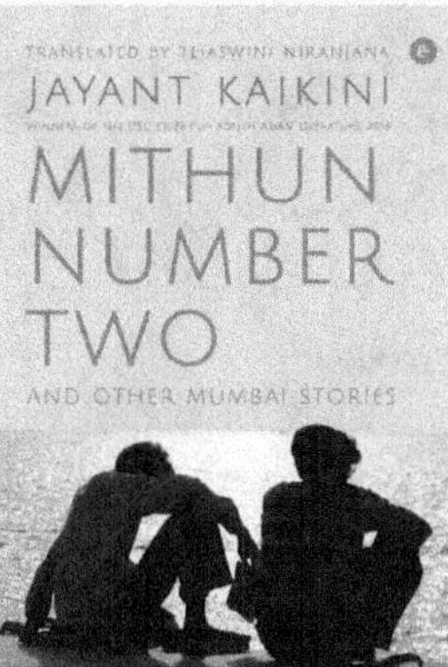

Also from ekadā

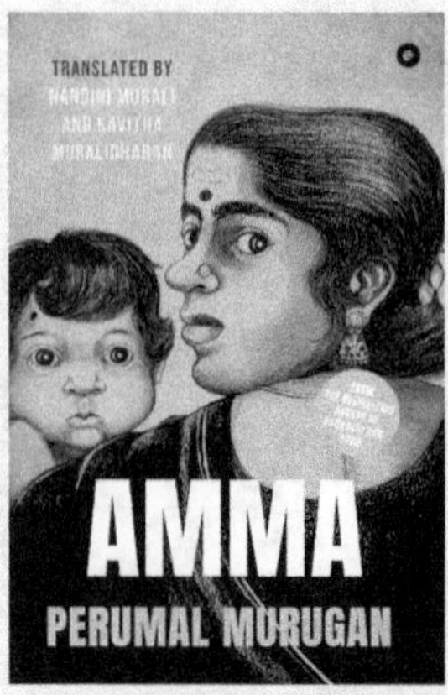